The Assassin
Fort Worth

Jim West

ISBN
Hardcover: 978-1-965134-01-6
Paperback: 978-1-965134-00-9

Other books by Jim West

DNAlien
DNAlien II
DNAlienIII
Genocide by GMO
Living Within a Strange Mind Volume I
Living Within a Strange Mind Volume II
The Making of an Assassin Atlanta
The Assassin Baltimore
The Assassin Chicago
The Assassin Denver
The Assassin El Paso

My special thanks to my oldest friend, John Fleenor, who has endured my clumsy attempts at literary work for too many years to remember. But his snide remarks keep me entertained while offering sound advice.
Thank you, John. Again.

Page Left Blank Intentionally

Chapter One

"Hello, Fort Worth, American Twelve Eighty-two is with you, passing Two Seven Zero for Two Three Zero," First Officer Jim Lashley said, checking on with Fort Worth Center as they descended for the landing at the Dallas Fort Worth Airport (DFW).

"American Twelve Eighty-two, continue the descent to six thousand, expect the visual to One Seven Center, DFW altimeter Three Zero Two Seven," the DFW approach controller directed.

"Down to six, one seven center, Three Zero Two Seven, American Twelve Eighty-two," Jim repeated as Captain Mark Moore pointed at his altimeter to verify the correct setting.

"Ladies and gentlemen, we'll be landing in approximately fifteen minutes," Mark announced. "Please return to your seats and keep your seatbelts fastened. Flight Attendants, prepare for landing."

"Your wife still picking you up when we get in?" Mark asked, hanging up the handset as he took a quick look at the DFW airport diagram.

"Yes, sir," Jim answered as he checked the arrival gate against his diagram also. "Seemed the fastest way to get to Fort Worth instead of me driving to the other side of Dallas just to turn around and drive back."

"Not to mention you guys are driving down to San Antonio tomorrow," Mark joked. "Wouldn't want ya'll to make the trip in that POS pickup you bring to the airport."

"No shit," Jim said, laughing. "Jennifer wouldn't ride five miles in my truck. She was talking to John and Mary, our friends down there, just before I left for this trip. I believe the conversation went something like, 'If Jim expects me to ride four hours in that old beat-up truck, you better not count on me coming with him when he gets there. Or even still be married to him.'"

"I understand," Mark agreed. "My ex wouldn't be seen in anything short of a Lexus. And even that couldn't be older than two years and fresh from the dealer's detailing."

"And you divorced her just for that?" Jim asked, laughing.

"No, it had more to do with finding out that the guy detailing the car was polishing more than the hood," Mark answered. "I knew that the car didn't need to be taken in twice a week. Hell, I bet she didn't drive it except to the dealer and back."

"Twice a week. Your garage must have been pretty dusty," Jim remarked, shaking his head. "Does she still have the car?"

"Mercedes," Mark answered, shaking his head. "Married the guy that owned the dealership."

"Well, at least she won't have to pay for getting her *car* detailed now." Jim said laughing. "And neither will you."

"She's his problem now. Where are you staying in Fort Worth?" Mark asked, rechecking his altimeter as they passed eighteen thousand.

"The Stockyards Hotel," Jim answered, pointing at his altimeter. "The restaurant there, the H3, has some of the best Huevos Rancheros I've ever had. That's one of the reasons for staying there. Plus, it's a short walk to some of the oldest bars and dance halls in Texas. Pretty touristy, but lots of fun."

"American Twelve Eighty-two, turn right to Two Zero Zero; the airport will be at your Twelve o'clock twenty miles, call it in sight," the controller told them as they approached ten thousand feet.

Seeing Mark nod that he had the airport, Jim answered, "Airport in sight."

"You're cleared the visual to One Seven Center, contact the tower One Twenty-six Fifty-five,'" the controller advised.

"Cleared the visual Seventeen Center, One Two Six Five Five," Jim replied as Mark hit the overhead chime.

"Tower, American Twelve Eighty-two, visual Seventeen Center," Jim said as he checked to the right for traffic on Seventeen Right.

"American Twelve Eighty-two, you're number one, cleared to land One Seven Center," the tower controller said.

"Cleared to land One Seven Center," Jim repeated as Mark called for the wing slats to be extended.

After landing, Jim switched to the terminal frequency after advising ground they were clear of the runway. As they made the turn into the area just yards from their gate, they were directed to hold while the aircraft on their gate was being pushed back.

As Mark was telling the passengers they were waiting for the gate to be clear, Jim acknowledged clearance to continue to the gate, tapped Mark's shoulder, and pointed, nodding his head.

Once parked and the engines were shutdown, Mark got out of his seat to say goodbye to the passengers as Jim verified that everything on the checklist had been accomplished before turning in his seat to watch.

Chapter Two

As the last of the passengers and the Flight Attendants from the coach section were leaving, Mark and Jim gathered their bags and joined Julie, the Flight Attendant who had worked first class and taken care of the cockpit for the trip.

"So, what are your plans for your days off?" she asked Jim as they headed up the jet bridge to the terminal.

"Vacation," he answered.

"Wish I could. How long will you be gone?" she asked as they approached the doors.

"Couple of weeks, but I won't have another trip until next month," he told her. "My wife and I are going to San Antonio for a few days; then we're taking a road trip down to Terlingua along with some old friends for a few more days to see the Big Bend country."

"That sounds like fun," she said, touching his arm. "When are you leaving?"

"My wife should be at the gate waiting for me," he told her as Mark pushed the doors open. "We'll spend the night in Fort Worth and then drive to my friend's house tomorrow."

"I'd like to meet the lucky lady that captured the infamous Jim Lashley," she said as she passed Mark as he held the door for them.

"Careful, infamous man," Mark whispered as Jim passed him. "I think this lady wants her car detailed."

As they entered the terminal, Jim saw Jennifer talking to the gate agent and walked toward her. "Hey honey, glad you got here on time. I've spent enough time in airport terminals these last couple of days."

"Oh, traffic wasn't too bad this time," she said as he sat his bags down and gave her a hug.

"This is Captain Moore," he said, introducing her. "He's the guy that's kept me out of trouble this month. I'm sure he'll be glad to get my replacement so he can relax and enjoy the rest of the month.

"Hi, Jennifer," Mark said, taking off his cap. "Please call me Mark. And don't listen to Jim. It's been a pleasure flying with him."

"Nice to meet you, Mark," Jennifer said, shaking his hand.

"And who is this beautiful lady?" she asked, turning to look at Julie.

"I'm Julie," she answered, offering her hand. "I had the pleasure of working with your husband and Captain Moore for the last three days. And I must say, these are two of the nicest pilots I've worked with in over 15 years."

"I'm not surprised," Jennifer told her. "Jim's Mom made sure he knew how to behave around ladies. And Jim has told me about Captain Moore. Sounds like his mother taught him some manners as well."

"Well, I've got to catch the tram to get my car and go home," Julie said as she started to turn away. "Nice to meet you, Jennifer. And I guess I'll see you next week, Captain Moore."

"Looking forward to it," Mark said as she was leaving. "Now, you guys are probably ready to get started as well."

"Jennifer, so nice to finally meet you," Mark said with a slight bow. "Jim, you treat this lady right. And hopefully, we'll get to fly together again before long."

"Good to meet you too, Captain Moore," Jennifer said, nodding.

"Please, just Mark," he said, picking up his bag. "You guys go enjoy yourselves while I stay here slaving on a hot airplane to get ungrateful people to undesirable locations."

"Take care, Mark. I'm sure I'll run into you again one of these days," Jim said as he picked up his bag. "Where'd you park, honey."

Chapter Three

Once they had checked in at the Stockyards Hotel, Jim suggested a walk along Exchange and visit a couple of the most well-known visitor attractions before the historic cattle drive reenactment scheduled for 4 o'clock that afternoon. The plan was to cross East Exchange and stop in at the White Elephant Saloon. And then head west to Miss Molly's.

"What's so special about the White Elephant?" Jennifer asked as Jim changed from his uniform into a pair of Wrangler jeans and a starched, long-sleeve white shirt.

Pulling on his Tony Lama boots, he explained, "The White Elephant saloon was, according to legend, the scene of the last gunfight in Fort Worth. The owner, a guy named Luke Short, who was supposedly a gunfighter from Dodge City, was being pressured by the Fort Worth sheriff, Jim Courtright, to pay 'protection' money."

"Short supposedly told Courtright to go to hell," Jim continued, "and that he could protect his business himself."

"The animosity escalated, and they met in front of the saloon where Short's first shot blew Courtright's thumb off, causing him to have to change hands with his pistol," Jim said as they headed for the door. "As he was trying to do it,

Short shot him again in the chest, killing him. He then shot him at least three more times just to make sure."

"Wow," Jennifer said as they headed downstairs. "And I suppose you are taking Short's side."

"Of course," Jim answered. "Courtright was a crooked Sheriff. Somebody had to do it."

"What about Miss Molly's? Why are we going there?" Jennifer asked as they came to the lobby.

"Miss Molly's was a well-known brothel," Jim explained as he started to open the door to go out onto the street. "Miss Josie was probably the best-known Madam. Her room was covered in red velvet, and she had a sign posted out front that, and I quote, 'Street ladies bringing in sailors must pay for a room in advance."

"Why sailors?" Jennifer asked as they stepped outside. "I wouldn't have thought there would be many sailors here anyway. I think I'd make them pay for the room in advance regardless of who they were *entertaining*,"

"I don't know," Jim answered as he looked left as they waited to cross the street. "Maybe the sailors were up here to ride with the cattle as they took them on the railroad to some port, maybe Houston."

As the light changed and they started across, Jim noticed a white Chevrolet sedan sitting about half a block west on Exchange. Not that cars parked along the street were uncommon, except this one looked the same as one that had been there when they had checked in.

There were at least two people sitting in the car as well. Again, it was not unusual if they were waiting for someone to come out of Miss Molly's Bed and Breakfast or the Star Café, which was beneath Miss Molly's.

As they crossed onto the other side of Exchange and were heading to the White Elephant, Jim heard the noise of an engine from behind him. Glancing back, he saw the white Chevrolet pulling away from the curb.

Still not overly concerned, he stepped to Jennifer's left to make sure he was between her and the street. They were almost to the White Elephant when he saw the car pulling up beside them.

Seeing the car in the reflection from the window of the White Elephant and seeing that there were at least four people in the car, he turned his head to look at it just as it came to a stop beside them.

As soon as he looked, he heard someone say, "Hey, Lashley," and saw three guns extend from the front and rear passenger windows of the car.

Pushing Jennifer to the ground, Jim dove on top of her as the shooters in the car began spraying his body with the fully automatic Uzis.

Within seconds, the car sped away, leaving Jim lying on top of Jennifer with blood covering her and running across the sidewalk. The last thing he heard was the squeal of the tires as the assassins fled.

Chapter Four

The first thing that Jim was conscious of was a slight humming noise and a hazy light. It seemed like he was just coming out of a dream or waking up.

The next thing was a thought running through his head: *Where's Jennifer? Where is she? Why isn't she here? Where is here? Where am I?*

Then came the realization that he couldn't move his head. He couldn't move anything. Not his arms, legs, maybe his fingers a little. As his eyes slightly opened, he realized that he was looking at a stranger. Moving his eyes back and forth, he tried to speak, but his jaw wasn't working.

Then the stranger leaned down and said something, more like a mumble, a blur of sound. As the stranger's head turned, the sound became more distinct. She, it was a her, was saying something to someone. Not him. She was looking away from him. Someone to her side.

As she moved out of his visual range, another face took her place. A familiar face, a man's face. Gene. General. He recognized him, General Gene Barker.

Then the man started to speak. At first, he didn't understand. Then the words became clear. The man, Gene, was calling his name.

"Jim, can you hear me?" General Barker was saying. "Do you understand me? Move your eyes if you can hear me."

Jim kept looking into Gene's eyes, wondering what he was doing there. Again, the thoughts, *where am I? Where's Jennifer? What's going on?*

"Jim, listen to me. If you can hear me, move your eyes to your left," Gene kept repeating. "Let me know that you understand."

Jim tried to say he understood, but nothing came out except a low grunt. Now terrified, his eyes darted back and forth from Gene to the space on the other side of his limited view.

Then another face appeared from his left, a man with a light that he kept shining in his eyes. "He's definitely awake," the man said. "Nurse, what do you see on the readouts?"

"His BP is elevated, his heart rate is rapid, his breathing is shallow and rapid," she replied. "And his EKG is all over the chart."

"That would be normal," the man said. "Let's give him a little something to calm him down for now.

"Nurse, give him two milligrams of Ativan in the IV and prepare one milligram of Geodon in a syringe and five milligrams of Haldol in case I need them," he directed.

Within a few seconds of the administration of the Ativan, Jim's blood pressure, heart rate, and breathing had returned to normal. "That should hold him for now," he told General Barker. "Let's see if you can get him to respond to some simple questions."

"Jim," Gene said quietly. "Don't try to talk for right now. Just blink if you understand."

Jim shifted his eyes to look at Gene's face and finally blinked.

"Good, that's very good," Gene said as he looked up at the doctor.

"You're in the Bethesda Naval Hospital in Washington DC," Gene told him. "You've been placed in a comatose state for over two weeks while the doctors have tried to take care of you. Do you understand?"

Jim's brow furrowed slightly as he stared at Gene's eyes. As he slowly comprehended what he'd been told, he again tried to speak and managed to barely whisper, "Jen?"

Gene looked at the doctor and waited until he nodded before saying, "She didn't make it."

Jim's eyes squeezed shut as a tear ran down each side of his immobilized face. Finally, he opened his eyes, blinking rapidly, looking from side to side. As his heart rate and blood pressure began rising, the doctor reached for the syringe and administered the drugs to his left shoulder.

A couple of minutes later, Jim's breathing had settled down, and the doctor said, "He's going to get a little groggy. Let's let him relax for a few minutes, and we'll try again. But it looks like he's starting to understand what's happening, and that's a good sign. We just have to wait to see what he remembers."

"I'm sorry, Jim," Gene said as he laid his hand on Jim's. "There was nothing we could do. I'm going to let you rest for now. The doctor will explain what happened and what they're doing for now. Just try to relax, and I'll be right outside when he's finished."

Chapter Five

As the doctor stepped from the room, Gene stood and asked, "What's your opinion, Doctor?"

"I can't be absolutely positive until we get a chance to run a few more tests, but I'd hazard a guess that any damage to his mental facilities is minor if any damage at all," the doctor said, crossing his arms. "There were no bullet fragments or other material that actually penetrated the skull. Lots of shrapnel from ricochets of surrounding surfaces, but it struck at such reduced energy that it inflicted very little damage except surface cuts and abrasion. At most, there may have been some concussion from their impact or as he fell."

"As to the rest of the damage to his body, only time will tell," he continued. "There'll undoubtedly be tremendous scarring and numerous issues from the 20-odd bullets that penetrated his organs and muscles."

"The splintered bones, another matter," the doctor stated. "Not unlike a broken bone, these will require time. We've done our best to rebuild them, but there's only so much we can do. We've harvested as much bone material from his hips and pelvis to repair his jaws and used the latest technology to wrap the mesh around other areas that will help replace the shattered bone and promote bone growth, but it's a very slow process."

"What's your best estimate for when he can get out of bed and move about, even if it's with assistance?" Gene asked. "Jim's not the type to just lie on his back for very long."

"Weeks," the doctor answered. "Possibly months. You've got to remember that both of his legs received major damage, and the bones simply will not support his weight at this point. Even with bone grafting, pins, and the mesh I was speaking of, it's going to be a long road to recovery…if ever. Amputation was always a millimeter away. What we're trying has never been attempted on this scale. He's lucky that he still has his legs and one of his arms."

"I understand, and I appreciate everything you and your teams have done," Gene said. "I just want you and everyone else to understand one thing explicitly…that young man is like a son to me. If there's any procedure, experimental or otherwise, that will return him to as much of a normal life as possible, do it. Cost is not a concern. "

"Black Water, the company I'm involved in, will cover any expense," Gene emphasized. "I'm not asking for you to bring him back to the physical state he was in before this happened; just give him a chance. I've known Jim for over 20 years, and I think you'll be surprised at how determined he can be."

"You folks have done a tremendous job already," Gene continued. "I'll be eternally in your debt. Now, all I'm asking is that you take the next step, even if it's only a leap of faith. If there's a procedure on the horizon that looks promising and, in your judgment, will improve his chances, let me know. I'll make sure it's available to you."

"I understand, General," the doctor replied. "I've done, and will continue to do, everything that's within the realm of possibility to get him back on his feet. Some of the procedures we're using on Jim may someday become standard practice and give another man a chance at a normal life."

"All these things I can do," he said, looking directly into Gene's eyes, "But the mental part, I can't control. I can recommend psychiatrists or psychologists, but it's up to Jim how he handles both the loss of his wife and the enormous physical damage he's suffered…and will continue to suffer for the remainder of his life. That's beyond my capabilities. That part is entirely in his hands."

"I'm not too worried about that part," Gene responded. "I'm pretty damn sure that he'll be able to take care of that issue without the assistance of psychiatrists, psychologists, voodoo medicine men from the Sub-Sahara, or a Shaman from some native tribe in any reach of the world. If I know my man, and I think I do, rage will take care of his will to resume his life. Not pity or group therapy…pure unadulterated rage.

I've worked with many men who can suffer injustice," Gene continued. "Men who have lost almost everything. Men who have given up on life and sat on their asses watching *Little House on the Prairie* or some other brain-numbing form of existence. Not Jim. Not by a long shot.

And when you toss in revenge, you've got a version of hell that's going to be straining at the bit to be released," Gene finished. "You take care of the physical issues; Jim will do the rest. Most people never see it, but there's a hidden, cold, calculating side to him. Where most people show their anger, Jim doesn't. But it's there just below a calm exterior. And when he starts thinking about what's been taken from him…his wife and his life as he knew it…hell will seem like paradise as to what he'll intend to do to those responsible. And I'll help him. Jennifer was as much a part of my family as Jim. Nobody hurts my family. No one. And I have the resources to ensure it's taken care of."

Chapter Six

Gene walked back into Jim's room and watched the nurse exchange one of the numerous bags of fluid that were providing nourishment and life-saving medicines to Jim's sedated body.

Waiting until she finished, he just stood quietly, looking at the broken body of his friend. Ever since he had encountered Jim on the battlefields in Vietnam, he had held a certain respect and connection to him. From recommending him for MARCAD (Marine Aviation Cadet), where he returned to Vietnam as an F-4 pilot, to recruiting him as an agent for Black Water, Gene had been his mentor for too many years to mention.

Now, with Jim's wife Jennifer gone and him barely clinging to life, Gene echoed the rage that he knew Jim held for those who had committed this atrocity against his world. But now was not the time to react. Now was the time to help Jim heal and provide whatever assurances he could that things would be made right.

As the nurse smiled and left, he stepped over to the bed and looked into the almost closed eyes that were the window to the inner man he realized he had almost lost. His own rage and need for revenge must be tempered with the desire to bring his friend back from the broken shell that lay unmoving on the bed in front of him.

Putting his hand on Jim's, he leaned over and softly said, "Hey, Marine. You got time for an old fellow Marine?"

As he saw Jim's eyes open slightly, he continued, "You're definitely a hard ass. I don't know of anyone who's gone through what you've just been through and lived to tell about it. Maybe it's just stubbornness. Hardheaded stubborn Marine.

Are you ready for me to tell you what's happening in the outside world?" Gene asked. "Just give me a blink."

As Jim slowly blinked, Gene nodded with a slight smile and said, "We know who did this. And trust me, they will be brought to justice. Right now, there's a team back at Black Water that's putting together a plan for retribution."

Jim's eyes opened wide, and he began to blink rapidly as he tried to speak. Through clenched teeth, he uttered a single word, "No."

Gene looked at the staring eyes and said, "I think I understand, and we'll get to that later."

Pausing for a second, Gene continued, "I know the doctor has talked about what damage you sustained and your chances for full recovery, but he doesn't know what happened to bring you to this point."

"We've been able to reenact the shooting through the videos we managed to get from all over the area in front of the White Elephant," Gene started.

"The folks in the photo interpretation division have analyzed everything down to the thousandth of a second," Gene explained. "From when the car left its parking spot up from where you were shot, we reconstructed the scene.

From when you first realized that something was wrong and put yourself between Jennifer and the street, we analyzed every bullet that was fired at you," he continued. "There were actually over 50 shots taken, 21 of which hit you or Jennifer. The others hit the building above you or ricocheted off the sidewalk.

It was one of those that ricocheted that killed Jennifer," he told Jim. "Several others passed through your body and hit her. But they weren't the fatal ones.

That one hit the sidewalk just below your neck and struck her in the side of her head," Gene explained. "You did everything you could to protect her. That one random bullet just happened to strike the only place where it could hit her without hitting you.

I just want you to understand what really happened," Gene said, leaning further over to look into his eyes. "You did everything you could.

Now, once the car sped away, it was mere seconds before an ambulance arrived," Gene continued as he leaned back. "Luckily, it was just down the block prepositioned for the four o'clock cattle drive up Exchange. If not for that, I'd have been attending two funerals instead of just one.

They loaded both you and Jennifer and headed toward downtown Fort Worth," he recounted. "Before they arrived at John Peter Smith, they had pronounced Jennifer dead, and you actually died three times before they arrived at the hospital.

The trauma surgeons began working on you as they wheeled you through the doors. The medics on the ambulance had used every drop of blood they had onboard and had told the hospital what to be expecting," Gene told him. "Even then, you actually died twice more before they finally stabilized you.

You were there for almost two weeks before they decided that you could be moved," Gene told him. "That's when I began coordinating between them and the doctors here at Bethesda Naval Hospital for your transfer."

"Excuse me, sir," the nurse said as she and two others entered the room. "You'll have to step out into the hall so we can take care of our patient. I'll let you know when you can come back in."

Chapter Seven

As the nurse exited Jim's room with her two assistants carrying what appeared to be sheets, blankets, and several trash bags with an assorted allotment of material inside, she paused to say, "You may go back in, but be aware that we'll be administering a little sleep aid in about an hour. After that, it'll be tomorrow morning before he'll be available."

"Thank you, Miss," Gene replied. "If there's anything I can do or not do to help you guys take care of my friend, please don't hesitate to let me know."

"I'll do just that," she paused and told him. "I know a lot about what that man has gone through. And I know that the odds are against him at this point. I had an uncle in Vietnam, and I know what that did to him. I understand that Mr. Lashley survived some very harrowing situations, as my uncle did. Trust me, those men and women will always get the most I can provide. Now, I've got other patients to care for."

As she walked away, Gene eased the door open to see nothing outward appeared to have changed. Stepping over to the bed, he saw that Jim's eyes were closed but were moving side to side beneath the lids.

As he put his hand on Jim's, he spoke softly and said, "I'm here for you, Marine. Now, tomorrow, and as long as I'm alive, I'll be here for you."

Jim's eyes eased open, and he looked to the side to meet Gene's and managed to eke out a barely audible "I know."

"Now, to bring you up to date on how I found out about what happened and how you got here," Gene told him. "But first, I know how difficult it is for you to speak. The doctor told me that a bullet had gone through your jaw taking out a sizable chunk of bone on each side. Then, they used a bone graft from your hips to replace the destroyed jawbone. Next, they wired everything together with some material between your remaining teeth so that you wouldn't break what they had reconstructed."

"Having said that, let's just stick to the blinks since your eyes are about the only things that aren't damaged," Gene suggested. "How about one blink for yes and two for no? Think you can manage that?"

A couple of seconds later, Jim blinked once, then pausing slightly, he blinked twice, then again blinked once.

Gene smiled and said, "Just as you've always been, never one to give an answer unless you know the question beforehand. I'll assume we have a gentlemen's agreement, but feel free to blink away to your heart's content if you are so inclined."

"How I found out," Gene started. "I'm sure you remember a lady who helped us out in El Paso. Named Bracer. Well, she's now a permanent part of Black Water. She was monitoring some electronic something or other, you know how she is, but heard your name mentioned."

"This alerted her, and then she heard the gunfire," he continued. "She immediately got a location and made a 911 call to the Fort Worth emergency hotline. When she found out the frequency the ambulance was using, she began monitoring that and found out where they were taking you, except she didn't know for sure it was you, but she did know there was also another victim, a female."

"The rest was easy," Gene said. "A couple of phone calls and we had the identities and a rough idea of what condition you were in. That's when I began making some inquiries into the best facility for your long-term care."

"Once JPS, or John Peter Smith, the hospital where you had been taken, confirmed your status, I had the company jet ready to fly me down to Carswell," he continued. "While there, I managed to find a company that would turn the plane into a flying ambulance to bring you up here as soon as the doctors down there released you."

"Now you're probably wondering why Bracer just happened to be listening to someone in Fort Worth," he offered. "Well, we've known for a couple of years that we had a leak within Dark Water."

"For some reason, several of our overseas contracts were being allowed to expire, and some of our bids were being rejected," Gene explained. "So we started trying to determine what had happened."

"That's when we brought in that tenacious little computer wizard. Within a couple of days, we had our answer…another contract enforcement company was underbidding us."

"That by itself wasn't the problem," Gene continued. "But it started the excavation process to figure out how they knew so much about our operations and could get the contracts."

"A few keystrokes later, we had the answer," Gene informed him. "One of our more senior operatives had decided to run his own version of Dark Water. He, Henry Lamance, had been with the company for almost ten years. He'd managed to get most of our so-called trade secrets and saw what he thought was an opportunity to build his own organization."

"Initially, he restricted himself mainly to small operations in some of the most undesirable countries," Gene explained. "These contracts weren't going to be that profitable for us to begin with, so we didn't pay close enough attention. But as the saying goes, once you've seen the lights of Broadway…"

"Then his operations start expanding," Gene said. "Contracts that we fully expected due to being a repeat provider suddenly disappeared. Long-term contracts that had been renewed numerous times were no longer extended."

"What Henry was doing, and we'd looked into the same thing years ago, was using indigenous mercenaries instead of company people," Gene told him. "The major cost of these operations is usually personnel. That's where Henry saw a huge profit opportunity. And it's a smart idea. Except that the loyalty of these people is uncertain, and leaks are abundant. And like a ship, enough leaks, and you'll sink."

"Anyway, Bracer began monitoring all of his electronic efforts and began building a fictitious company," Gene explained. "To be sure we were on the right track, I gathered the heads of all the departments, and we developed a proposal for an operation in Mogadishu. With instruction to keep it only at department head level requesting budgetary input, we waited to see if he acted."

"Within two days, he was reaching out to a high-level official in Mogadishu asking if there were any opportunities for his operation," Gene said smiling. "That's when we knew we had the right guy."

"Once we began monitoring both him and any of his contacts, it became clear that he was going to try and start a domestic operation parallel to our Muddy Water ops," Gene continued. "His basic plan to use indigenous mercenaries was still at the heart of his operational plan, but he had one major stumbling block…he couldn't compete with our people."

"That brings us to what we believe is his plan to level the playing field," Gene said with a glare in his eyes. "He plans on eliminating the majority of our top operatives. Those he's known about since he started with Black Water."

"You just happened to be the first. At least as far as we've determined," Gene continued. "We've notified everyone who has ever run a major operation or been instrumental in its implementation that the threat is real. We've got enough data to provide our people with a portfolio of suspected operatives' photos, and Bracer has a staff of over 100 who are monitoring everything so we can get as much advance notice as possible of their next target."

"One major problem has surfaced," he explained. "Henry knows all about Bracer's voice recognition programs. And her location programs are based on cell phones. To counter these, he's using a single-use phone and electronically changing their voices when using the phones."

"What the asshole doesn't know is that our lady of the Ethernet has perfected a voice recognition program that looks at the cadence of a person's dialogue and matches it with certain terms or words that an individual commonly uses," he continued. "Such as a man who says 'As I've said' or 'Know what I mean' or pauses with an 'uh' too often, or something similar, the computer figures out who it was and our friends at the National Security Agency, or NSA, have incorporated her program into their systems. Bingo, we're back in the saddle again."

Looking at his watch, Gene finally said, "I know I've probably tranquilized you more than those shots the doctors and nurses have been giving you by now, so I'll leave before they get back here, and I'll come back in the morning, and we'll discuss how we're going to take care of this little issue."

Just as he was turning to leave, the nurse came in saying, "Sorry, General. Time to put our man to sleep. I'd suggest you probably need a little shuteye yourself, from the looks of your eyes, and knowing how much time you've been sitting here over the last week or so. You scoot on back to wherever you're staying and try to get some rest."

"Yes, ma'am," Gene said, turning to wink at Jim. "I just happen to have a bottle of brain relaxer back in my room. See you tomorrow, Marine. Semper Fi."

Chapter Eight

The following morning, Gene was waiting outside Jim's room when the doctor came out. "Good morning, doctor," he said. "How's our boy doing?"

Looking up from the folder he was carrying, the doctor answered, "Pretty good. We took him down this morning for a full regiment of MRIs, a CRT, and X-rays. The bone mass in most of the areas has increased at a higher rate than we originally anticipated. And that's a very good sign."

"You say most," Gene questioned. "Does that mean there are areas that aren't gaining mass?"

"No, definitely not," the doctor answered. "There are a couple that are pretty much on track for our expectations; the rest are gaining faster. I'm not sure what's causing the increased bone mass growth in those areas, possibly blood flow, since some areas had more soft tissue damage than others, but I'm going to see if I can figure it out. I'd like to try to replicate the growth pattern in those other areas."

"Good," Gene said, nodding. "When do you think you can start letting him have some increased movement? I'm sure he'd like to be able to turn his head or move his jaw so he can speak."

"Probably within the next couple of days," the doctor answered. "The jaw bones are one of the areas of increased bone mass production, so I believe we can start there. He'll have to be on a liquid diet for another week or so, even if we take out the wires as a precaution against breaking the bones we repaired. Then soft foods for a couple of weeks before we start replacing the teeth that were destroyed when the bullet passed through his face."

"And his neck?" Gene asked. "What about that so he can at least turn his head?"

"Probably about the same," he answered. "I'd like to start slowly, as with the jaw and neck, before we even think about the arms or legs. The bones there will probably need another month before we let him put any strain on them. They're big bones, but they'll have to support a lot of weight. We'll put a cast on his arms where the breaks occurred, and he can begin some light exercises, such as squeezing a tennis ball, but his legs are another matter."

"That's at least some good news," Gene replied as he thought about how difficult it was going to be for Jim during the next couple of months. Not to mention the months of therapy before he could return to a halfway normal life.

"Yes, it's very good news," the doctor said as he closed the folder. "Now, I've got other patients to see this morning. Have a good day, General."

As he turned toward the door, it swung open, and a nurse carrying several IV fluid bags came out. "Excuse me, ma'am," Gene said. "Is it safe for me to go in?"

"You'll need to wait a few more minutes," she answered. "They're replacing the catheter and the colostomy bag."

"Could you do me a favor while I'm waiting?" he asked, smiling.

"Certainly, if I can," she replied. "What would you like me to do?"

"Can you get me an IV bag with yellow fluid and another with brown fluid?" he asked. "I'd like to play a little joke on Jim."

"I think I can manage that," she said. "I'll just use two of these empty IV bags. I'll be right back."

When she returned a couple of minutes later, she handed him the bags and asked, "Just what kind of joke are you planning?"

Gene grinned and held up the brown and yellow filled bags, saying, "Bacon and eggs."

Shaking her head, she walked off, muttering, "Marines. Navy. Air Force. Any military. A strange sense of humor."

Gene nodded at the two people leaving the room and saw that Jim's eyes were fully open. Stepping up to the bed on the side where the IV bags were hanging, he said, "Good morning, Marine. Breakfast. I know you're quite partial to C rations or, better yet, shit on a shingle, but these scrambled eggs and bacon are the best I could do on short notice."

As he hung the bags, he saw Jim roll his eyes, and a noticeable exhalation escaped his mouth. Smiling to himself, Gene knew his friend would pull through. Even a small sign of Jim's old personality gave him hope.

Chapter Nine

Three months later, as Jim was pushed from the hospital in a wheelchair, Gene stood waiting in the street beside an electric cart much like the ones used on golf courses around the country.

"You're going to drive me down to Quantico with that POS?" Jim asked as the attendants helped him out of the wheelchair.

"Most certainly, except you'll be the one driving. I must get back to work, so I don't have time," Gene said, smiling as he took Jim's right arm. "This is about as fast as the doctor said you can travel. I know it's a step down from the F-4, but adjustments must be made for the handicapped and invalids."

"And I suppose you're going to take the helicopter I see sitting there on the pad," Jim responded, taking a cautious step toward the cart.

"Rank? Privileges? You remember those little niceties?" Gene quipped, helping Jim onto the cart. "You think you deserve some consideration because you've been pampered for the last few months?"

"Pampered? Having tubes stuck up every orifice in your body? And some that were cut into you just so they could shove another tube or something inside you? If that's pampering, give me a sadomasochistic ex-wife living in my spare room with the only TV remote," Jim replied as Gene slipped behind the wheel.

"Well, if it's that important to you, I'll let you ride with me in the chopper," Gene told him as they headed to the waiting helicopter. "Anyway, I don't think your Texas driver's license is still valid. Especially here in Washington DC."

As soon as they were strapped into the rear seats, the pilot started the engines, and they soon slipped into the morning sky. "Now I believe I'm free again," Jim said as they headed south. "There were times I thought I'd never get out of there."

"It's still going to take a little more time," Gene said as the Washington Monument came into view. "But the Gunny Sergeant that's going to be working with you will make sure you're back on your feet, so to speak, as fast as your body allows."

"When do I get to start working on Operation Retribution?" Jim asked. "My body may need some slight tweaking, but my mind is fully up to speed."

"We have a little welcoming party planned for this afternoon," Gene answered. "You'll be meeting some of the new people and several you already know. These are the folks that have been keeping track of our targets."

"I suppose Bracer will be there as well," Jim said.

"Most definitely," Gene assured him. "She's been anxious to see you since she made the 911 call almost six months ago."

"I appreciate the welcoming party, and I'm looking forward to seeing everyone, but when do I actually get to go to work?" Jim asked.

"Tomorrow, you're going to spend most of the day with all of the paperwork to start your new life," Gene reminded him. "I've got a team of personnel that will guide you through most of that. The guys from financial will go thru the accounts we established for your salary that started on the day you were shot."

"And, by the way, I talked to Bob Crandall the other day, and even though you've exhausted all of your sick days with American, he gave me his personal guarantee that as soon as the company doctors are satisfied with your physical status, they'll issue you a new FAA Class I medical," Gene informed him. "Your original employee number is still valid, and they'll begin retraining as soon as you receive your bid." "Have you notified the folks you rented my house to that I'll be coming back?" Jim asked.

"Yes, I gave them their 30-day notice this morning," Gene answered. "I don't think you'll be ready in 30 days, but the movers will bring all of your household goods back as soon as the renters are out, and the place cleaned."

"As much as I appreciate everything you've done for me, I'm ready to get back to Texas," Jim told him as the Marine Corps Base Quantico came into view. "I need to be back in my house so I can start letting go of Jennifer. I know she's gone, but it still feels like I need to go home to see her."

"I understand," Gene said as the helicopter began its descent for landing. "It took months before I stopped looking for my wife after she died. Every time I walked into the house; I'd listen for her voice. Every time I walked into the kitchen, I looked to see if she was there at the stove. Even today, there are times that I hear her fussing around somewhere in the house. Picking up something. Doing just about anything that a normal wife would be doing. Sometimes, I'll mute the TV and listen. I expect the same will happen with you."

Chapter Ten

As soon as they had landed and gotten into the black Suburban that came to get them, they drove straight to the Black Water Headquarters from the flight line.

Once inside the secured area that surrounded the nondescript concrete building, the driver let them out in front of the main entrance. Showing his badge upon entering the small enclosure where a guard sat checking everyone's identification against an access list, once cleared, Gene led them into the interior and down a hall to one of the large briefing rooms.

As Jim entered through the door Gene was holding open, he was greeted by dozens of people standing beneath a large banner that read "Welcome Back Marine."

Several of them came forward smiling, welcoming him back. As they congratulated him on his swift recovery, they returned to a banquet table where an array of finger foods was waiting. Finally wandering to the bar, Gene ordered a Jack and Coke, asking Jim what he wanted.

"A Jack and Coke sounds good to me right now," Jim said, leaning up against the bar.

Just as the bartender was handing him his drink, he heard a woman's voice behind him saying, "You wouldn't believe how good it is to see you still alive."

Turning, Jim stood looking at a smiling Bracer and finally said, "And I believe that I owe that to you."

"I'm just so sorry that I couldn't do more for Jennifer," she said with tears forming in the corners of her eyes. "I almost couldn't stand to hear the gunfire after I heard them call your name. I'm so sorry."

"There wasn't anything more you could have done," Jim said, putting his hand on her arm. "I'm just thankful you were there and made the quick call that saved me. Another minute or two waiting for someone else to react would have meant my life, also. So, thank you."

"Now, when do we start to work?" Jim asked, tilting his head to the side.

Debbie leaned in close and whispered, "We'll be meeting tomorrow. This isn't the place to discuss anything. Gene is bringing in everyone that needs to be involved in the morning."

"Good," Jim replied. "Have there been any more, let's say, incidents?"

"Again, tomorrow," she answered. "But we've been lucky."

Gene turned from speaking to one of the men wearing the customary black knit shirt with the Black Water logo over the pocket and told them, "We'll be in this room tomorrow. Breakfast will be set up at eight o'clock, and I'm hoping we'll be done before lunch. Are you ready, Debbie?"

"Yes, sir," she replied. "I'll be here at seven with my team, and we'll set everything up. Unless there are any questions from the few people that'll be attending the briefing, I should be done by about ten."

"Good," Gene told her, looking around at the thinning crowd. "I'm going to take Jim over to his quarters and let him rest. If he leans any harder on the bar, it may collapse."

"I'm good," Jim argued. "Just relaxing."

"Sure thing," Gene replied. "Then let's say that I'm tired and need to rest. You're just unlucky enough that I'm your escort until we get you some new identification."

Jim pushed himself away from the bar and told Debbie, "Guess I'll see you tomorrow. If you aren't too busy after the briefing, I'd like a little time to ask some questions that I don't think need to be brought up in an open discussion."

"No problem," she answered. "We can meet in my office after the brief is over. Is there anyone else you'd like to attend?"

Jim turned to Gene and asked, "Would you like to join us, sir?"

"I probably should," he answered. "I'm fully aware that something has been swirling around in your mind for the last few weeks. Just don't get too anxious. Until the Gunny says you're fit, you'll just have to be content to sit at a desk."

Chapter Eleven

The following morning, there was a Suburban sitting outside of Jim's temporary residence when he walked out of the Bachelor Officer's Quarters.

Ignoring the rear seat door the driver was holding open, he walked to the front passenger door, opened it, and said, "I'd rather sit in the front, Sergeant, if you don't mind."

"Not at all, Colonel," the Sergeant said, getting into the driver's seat.

"Please, just call me Jim," he said as he buckled his seatbelt. "Hopefully, I won't be too much of an inconvenience for you."

"Not at all, Colonel," the Sergeant said, letting Jim know that he would use the rank as a matter of respect instead of using his first name as requested. "And if there's ever anything you need from me, please don't hesitate to let me know. Until you're transferred out, I'm at your disposal."

"How do I get in touch with you?" Jim asked as they headed toward the isolated area that encompassed the Black Water Headquarters.

"Just call the motor pool," the Sergeant answered as they pulled into the first checkpoint. "The number is in the directory on the desk back in your room. They can transfer your call directly to me."

"That sounds great," Jim told him as the guard handed him a package, including a temporary ID badge, and the gate in front opened, allowing them to continue to the building. "I hope I won't be staying here much longer."

"As long as I'm needed, I'll be available," he replied as they arrived at the front of Black Water Headquarters. "I'll be back at the motor pool when you need to head home."

"Guess I'll see you after lunch," Jim said as he got out of the car and headed up the sidewalk.

As he handed his ID to the guard in the cubicle that controlled access to the interior, the door opened, and Gene stepped in, saying, "I've got him, Ronald. Tell the front gate thanks for letting me know he was here."

"How was your evening?" Gene asked, leading them to the conference room.

"Extremely exciting," Jim said as they walked in. "There was a *Gunsmoke* marathon on TV until five and then a *Little House on the Prairie* marathon after that. I finally found a home shopping network and watched it until I gave up and went to bed."

"You didn't find little Carrie's antics entertaining?" Gene asked as they headed for the breakfast buffet table.

"Captivating," Jim answered as he filled his plate with scrambled eggs, bacon, and hash browns. "I'm hoping it's still running this evening when I get back."

"I could have a cactus plant sent over," Gene smirked. "You could watch it grow instead."

"Make it a hanging fern," Jim told him as they took seats at the front of the room. "At least I can push it and watch it swing."

As they were setting their plates on the table, Debbie walked up to the podium, looked at her watch, and announced, "I'm about ready to get this started, folks. Please get whatever you want and take a seat."

"Still a little blunt, isn't she," Jim whispered, leaning over to Gene. "Guess some things never change."

"I believe she thinks she's actually being patient," Gene replied. "I've heard that she actually chastises her computer when it doesn't give her an answer fast enough."

"Lotta strange ducks in the Ethernet Pond," Jim mused, looking at the people taking seats.

"Walks like a duck, talks like a duck…" Gene replied.

As a list of names appeared on the screen behind her, Debbie said, "If you please pay attention, I'll try to get through this as fast as possible so we can all get back to work."

Turning slightly to look at the screen, she continued, "Here are all of the people we are currently tracking. The three shifts of our folks have someone dedicated to ten of them 24 hours a day. These 60 names are also being closely monitored by the NSA using the latest voice recognition profiles. Their computers are tied with ours to ensure we get immediate updates."

Pausing as everyone looked at the list, she continued, "Once we get a new phone number, our teams insert a virus into that phone, and we begin tracking and recording any conversation within approximately 50 feet, depending on the surrounding noise levels."

"Even though these people have been directed to only use their phones for company business and to destroy them after a single use, most of them have kept at least one for personal use after supposedly destroying it," she said with a slight smile.

"Sometimes we know what they are saying on their new phone before the NSA sends it to us; since the old phone is usually still on their person, we can hear their conversation on the other phone," she said. "That's actually a good thing for us because we can track them before they use their new phone, and we can program it."

"Also, we get to hear other operatives when they don't realize that we're listening," she continued. "We've learned more from that than the actual phone conversations on the supposedly clean phones."

"An additional note on their elaborate code scheme," she told them. "With all of the technology available today, they still seem to be using what I refer to as a decoder ring."

"The best example I can give is if you remember the Little Orphan Annie secret decoder ring Ralph got for sending in a gazillion Ovaltine labels in *A Christmas Story*," she told them, shaking her head. "We've managed to reconstruct their version of an Enigma machine and probably know the message before they do."

"We've been lucky so far," she continued. "We've managed to intercept their communications and informed our people, their targets, before anything like the attack on Jim Lashley could occur again. But we have to be correct a hundred percent of the time. They only have to succeed once, and we'll have failed."

"Now, if there are no questions, I'd like to thank everyone for coming this morning, and I suggest we all get back to work," she said as she turned and walked away from the podium.

"I guess there weren't going to be any questions," Jim said, watching her leave.

"Never is," Gene told him. "I don't think anyone wants to hear her answer and be berated for even asking such an obvious question. Now, if you're finished, I told Debbie we'd be in her office as soon as this briefing was over, which it is since she's left the room."

"Let's not keep her waiting," Jim said as he rose. "As the old saying goes, a blunt knife cuts more than a sharp blade."

"Whoever said that, and what does it have to do with this?" Gene asked as they left.

"Not sure, and probably nothing," Jim answered. "Maybe my great-great-grandfather said it many years ago."

"Sometimes I wonder about you," Gene said as they walked down the hall to Debbie's office.

"Is that another way of saying I'm a wonder?" Jim remarked, smiling.

"Not at all," Gene replied as they approached her door. "Not at all."

Chapter Twelve

"Come in, gentlemen," she said as they knocked on her door. "Please, have a seat."

Taking seats on the couch that faced two chairs across a small table, Gene said, "Thanks for taking time for us this morning. I know you're busy, and we'll try to keep this as short as possible."

"No problem," she said, sitting in one of the chairs across the table from them. "Would you like something to drink?"

"Black coffee would be great," Jim answered. "And I echo Gene's thanks. I'm sure some of the things I want to discuss couldn't be brought up in front of the general population of your department, or anywhere else except in private with you and Gene."

"That's why I'm here," she said as she asked her secretary to bring a carafe of coffee.

Waiting until the tray had been set on the table in front of them, she asked the secretary to close the door and then said, "Again, Jim, "I'm so terribly sorry about Jennifer. I wish we had known about how far Henry had gone with his effort to remove most of our top people before this happened. I still don't know what he thinks he was going to accomplish."

"My guess is that he thought he'd disrupt our organization long enough to get a toe hold on the domestic side as he did overseas," Gene mused. "With his prior experience in the company, he knew how much we depended on our senior agents to run most operations autonomously. Removing them would have had a major impact on the number of operations we could run simultaneously."

"I'm not too terribly interested in why he did shit," Jim told them angrily. "I couldn't care less. That bastard took something from me that can't be replaced, and how the company wants to handle the problem isn't my concern. For me, this is personal."

Seeing both Debbie and Gene waiting, he continued, "What has he got? Fifty or sixty operatives? The company can do whatever it wants with those people. Lamance is mine. As are the driver and the shooters who were involved with killing Jennifer."

"The company can either help me find these people and then stand aside while I visit some evil on them, or I'll do it on my own," he told them. "I still have enough friends across the country with the company that I'm pretty damn sure they'd be willing to provide me with enough information to find these people."

"You know you have the full support of the company," Gene told him. "Debbie's been working tirelessly developing a program that traces these people specifically. My only request is that you let me know what your plans are and when you'll implement them."

"I agree with the General," Debbie said, leaning forward. "But we need to be kept in the loop since we'll be running simultaneous operations with the others. You'll be given all of the information we have, but we need to de-conflict whatever you're doing with our operations."

"Just what are your plans?" Gene asked. "Some shootout at the OK Corral? A repeat of something like the Saint Valentine's Day massacre?"

Pausing for a second, he continued, "You might want to be a lone wolf for this. Especially knowing how personal it is to you. But you do have some limitations. Not just in the intelligence area, but you still have some issues with your physical condition. I'm asking you to sit back for a while and let us develop a plan that'll accomplish what you want and what's best for the company as well."

"We aren't interested in retribution of the people Henry recruited for his organization," Gene told him. "They were just acting in their own self-interests. Unfortunately for them, they chose poorly for their own futures within the security community. They'll be lucky if they can find a job as mall cop after we spread the word."

Debbie rose from her seat, got a package from her desk, and handed it to Jim, saying, "Gene asked me to put this together for you. Here's everything we have on Henry and the other people you're interested in. There's also a phone that's connected to our computers, and it has been encrypted, so any communications either by you using it or if it's picking up conversations as we have on their phones, it'll be unintelligible to anyone listening."

"We don't think they have that capability yet," Gene added. "But we're not taking any chances. Henry has been getting better at getting information, and we still think we have someone else within the organization that's helping him. But that's not your problem."

"I'm sure I'll know who it is within a week," Debbie promised, nodding. "But in the meantime, please use the phone for any communications. I'd prefer face-to-face, but I know you have another life you need to get back to, and my time for meetings is rather sparse as well."

"Speaking of time, we need to let you get back to work, and Jim has an appointment with his physical therapist," Gene said, standing. "Again, thank you for seeing us this morning, and I'm sure you'll be letting us know if anything changes regarding Jim's interests."

"That's a given," Debbie said, standing and offering Jim her hand. "And my door is always open for either of you. This hasn't impacted me nearly as personally as it has you, Jim. But it's still a priority to me to be there for you with anything you need."

"Thank you," Jim said, shaking her hand. "I appreciate everything you've done for me and Jennifer. She may not have agreed with what I'm about to do, and you may not either, but I know I have a better chance at success with you at my back. So, thank you again."

Chapter Thirteen

"Let's go to the Officer's Club for lunch," Gene suggested as they left Debbie's office. "Then I'll take you back to your room so you can get your gym clothes for your afternoon therapy. How's that going?"

"Pretty good," Jim answered as they headed for Gene's car. "The Gunny's a little too concerned about pushing me too hard, but I explained that even though I'm not as young as his recruits back when he was a Drill Instructor, I'm very well aware of my own limitations and I'll decide when I'm at my limit for the day."

"I understand your desire to be back to work and to take care of Lamance," Gene told him as they pulled into the parking lot. "But I also know how much damage you suffered and how long the doctors say it'll probably be until you're fully recovered. At least as much as you'll ever recover."

"And don't forget that you have another appointment with the folks up at Bethesda next week," he continued as they headed inside. "With luck, they'll give you a clean bill of health on how your insides have healed. But don't expect the same for your leg bones. Those could take another few months before they say the bones have regained enough mass for strenuous activity.”

“I know,” Jim said as they took their seats at the table. “I was there. And I also know what the doctor said about pressure on a bone to stimulate growth. Trust me. I can feel it when I’m pushing too hard. That’s something neither the Gunny nor the doctors can do.”

As soon as the waiter had taken their order, Gene asked quietly, “What are your plans once you decide it’s time?”

Glancing around to ensure they couldn’t be overheard, Jim answered, “Pretty simple for the driver and the guys that actually did the shooting. That’s going to be as quick and simple as I can make it. Probably a shot to the side of their heads just as they did to Jennifer. It's sort of an Old Testament-style thing. You know, an eye for an eye.”

“And Henry?” Gene asked.

“I’m still working on that,” Jim told him. “I’ve got to make a few calls and a visit to an old friend when I get back to Texas.”

“What do you need from us?” Gene asked.

“Pretty much the same as I needed in El Paso,” Jim answered. “Locations, number of people around, means of access, pretty much anything that will put me within a foot or so of the target with little possibility of being seen or caught on camera.”

“We can do most of that,” Gene said as their orders were placed on the table. “What about equipment?”

“Access to a disposable car would be nice,” Jim said as he tried his Caesar salad. “Probably more than one if there’s any chance of it being seen and associated with any of the other events.”

“That would probably be the case since we can’t guarantee the people or person involved would be in your vicinity when you need to meet with them," Gene agreed, nodding. "That can be arranged as soon as we know when you're ready and where you need to go."

"What about transportation if it's not in my local area?" Jim asked.

"I'll have to look at that when it needs to be done," Gene answered, slicing off a piece of his prime rib. "My initial inclination is to use the company jet. But we may need a smaller airplane if it's in a more remote area that doesn't have a sufficient runway or refueling capability."

"I'll also need a cold piece to use each time," Jim continued as he took a sip of iced tea. "I don't want anything that would tie any of these events together. I even want the ammo to be from different manufacturers if not different caliber equipment to use each time."

"Anything else?" Gene asked.

"For the first four, that's about it," Jim answered, finishing his steak.

"I'm assuming you have a different plan for the remainder," Gene replied, placing his napkin on the table and signaling for the bill.

"Very much so," Jim told him. "All I need from you is the location and approach. I'll have everything else necessary."

"I'm assuming that's why you need to make a few calls and visit an old friend when you get home," Gene suggested as they headed out.

"You'd be correct," Jim acknowledged. "I'll know more about what I may need once I get with him."

"I suppose you don't want to tell me what you're planning," Gene said as they walked to the car.

"No," Jim answered. "Maybe sometime. Maybe never. All you really need from me is proof that the man no longer exists. How I arrange that is irrelevant as far as the company is concerned."

"Have you ever heard of 'Lingchi'?" Jim asked, getting in the car.

"If you're talking about the Chinese execution by torture, known more commonly as death by a thousand cuts, yes, I have," Gene answered as they headed for Jim's room.

"It was supposed to have been abolished back in the early 1900s," he continued. "However, it was occasionally being used during the Korean war in the 50's and even as late as Vietnam."

"Sometimes a man must reach deep within the depths of inhumanity," Jim said as he got out of the car. "Sometimes even that's not enough to satisfy the wrong that has been done."

Chapter Fourteen

Six weeks later, as Jim was watching the movers bringing all of his belongings back into the house he had shared with Jennifer for so many years, a black Suburban pulled up to the curb outside his house in Mesquite, Texas.

After telling one of the guys to bring a box into the house and where to put it, he turned when he heard footsteps coming through the front door. Seeing Gene standing just inside, he smiled and said, "Don't just stand there. Go grab a box, and I'll tell you where to put it."

"I'm sure you'd love to tell me where to put it," Gene said, walking to him with his hand outstretched. "How are you doing?"

"Fine, I guess," Jim admitted, shaking Gene's hand. "I forgot just how much crap I'd accumulated over the years."

"It really adds up," Gene agreed. "I think a man should go through every closet, drawer, box, countertop, and crevice in his house at least once every three years and toss everything he hasn't used since the last purge."

"You know, I used to do pretty much the same thing when I was still in the Marines," Jim replied. "Since they moved me about every three years, I'd watch the movers packing, and I had a space on the floor in each room for them to put stuff I didn't want to take with me. But by the time I moved again, I needed another purge, as you call it."

"How are things with American since you passed your FAA physical?" Gene asked, looking around at the unopened boxes.

"I'm supposed to start retraining on the Super 80 in three days," he answered as he pointed to the kitchen for one of the workers carrying a box. "That'll take about a month. Then I have to get what's called an Initial Observation Evaluation, or IOE. That's normally a three-day trip with one of the Check Airmen."

"Last time, it took almost a month for the IOE," Jim continued. "So, I just sat around until they called and told me when to be at the airport. I hope it goes a little faster this time."

"How's the moving back into the house going?" Gene asked, watching guys carrying furniture through the door.

"So far, not bad," Jim replied. "I guess the thing I'm not looking forward to will be unpacking all of the boxes. I'd be willing to bet that three-quarters of those going to the bedroom are full of Jennifer's stuff."

"I'm sure you're right," Gene told him, putting his hand on Jim's shoulder. "That's going to be the toughest part."

"Right now, I don't know what I'll do with her stuff," Jim admitted, shaking his head. "I feel like I'm throwing part of her away if I just throw it in the trash. And I know I can't stand having her stuff sitting around reminding me of her every day. I'm not sure exactly what I'll do with it."

"Well, that's not a decision you need to make right now," Gene said. "It took me almost a year to make my decision. In the end, I gave it to the Salvation Army because that was one of her favorite charities. I damn sure didn't want to give it to anyone that I'd run into and see her favorite dress or necklace on some other woman."

"I'm sure you didn't come all this way just to talk about household goods," Jim said a few seconds after turning from watching the movers. "Is there something specific you wanted to talk about?"

"Let's go outside," Gene said, nodding. "If they need instructions, they can come get you by my car."

As Jim leaned against the front fender, Gene said, "The company has decided that they won't take any action against anyone who was involved with Henry unless they were former Black Water employees or otherwise involved with any part of an active attempt on one of our people."

"I can understand the wisdom in that," Jim agreed. "How many ex-Black Water people are we talking about?"

"Only ten," Gene answered. "They were all involved with Henry on various operations over the years he worked with Dark Water."

"Were any of them involved in attempting to take any of our people out?" Jim asked.

"Not that we know of," Gene told him. "We've been reviewing all of the communications previous to your shooting to see if we could tie them to any part of it. Even if they were only involved in the planning, we would be taking some punitive measures. But Henry appears to have only been using them on a couple of contracts he had acquired here in the States."

"And before you ask, those that were involved with any part of your shooting, even the planning, are going to be dealt with when you're ready," Gene said.

"You must know that with the training and the IOE, it'll probably be a couple of months before I can do anything," Jim told him.

"I figured as much," Gene said. "That's not a problem. We keep gathering more data on the people you're interested in as well as those we are. That'll give us more information on them and make it easier to conduct our business once you're ready."

"What about the inside leak you thought you still had?" Jim asked.

"Debbie found him a week after we were talking about it," Gene answered. "We've left him in place and are running a little misdirection program with him. He'll be the last shoe to drop, shutting down Henry's operations. As long as he doesn't know he's being used, we can maneuver Henry and his crowd somewhat as we want."

"What about me?" Jim asked. "I'm sure he knows by now that he failed to eliminate me. What's his plan for me?"

"That's one of the things that our leaker is helping us with," Gene answered. "We've convinced him through intercompany memos and other communications that you've retired and are no longer associated with any branch of Black Water."

"We even had a retirement ceremony planned and had to cancel it because you refused to come back," Gene told him, laughing. "The next morning, he contacted Henry and relayed the information to him. Henry's response was, 'At least he's gone, and we don't have to waste time or resources on him'".

"You may be convinced," Jim told him. "But I still jump at every sound. I turn and look at every car I hear coming up behind me or stare at the ones coming toward me from the front."

"Honestly, I don't think you need to worry," Gene advised him. "I certainly understand how you feel. But we're monitoring Henry and his folks so closely that we know when they flush the toilet and whether or not they washed their hands."

"I won't stop worrying until I watch him die," Jim said, shaking his head. "Then I can also tell Jennifer that I killed the sorry bastard that took her life."

Chapter Fifteen

Almost a month later, Jim had just gotten home after finishing his last day of training at the Flight Academy when the phone rang. Hoping it was Crew Scheduling calling him to arrange his IOE, he answered, "Hello."

"Good afternoon, Jim," came the familiar voice of Gene. "Would you like to go out for dinner and a drink to celebrate finishing the schoolhouse?"

"I'd ask how you knew that," Jim answered, smiling. "But I've come to expect you to know what I'm doing every second of every day. Whatever happened to personal privacy?"

"You signed a waiver the first day you joined Black Water," Gene answered. "Now, would you like to go to dinner with an old friend and have a couple of drinks, or do you have better plans?"

"I'm always at your disposal, General. And could never possibly have better plans than enjoying your company," Jim told him, checking the time. "How long until you can get here?"

"Look out your door," Gene told him. "How long until you can get here?"

"Give me five minutes, and I'll be on my way," Jim replied, smiling.

"Five minutes, Marine," Gene said. "Clock's running."

After shutting his door and walking down the sidewalk to the usual black Suburban Gene preferred, he got in the passenger door and asked, "Where do you plan on taking me for dinner since you extended the invitation?"

"It seems that I remember a little family-run pizza parlor not far from here that you frequented before you took a year off to lay around," Gene answered as he pulled from the curb. "Is that suitable for you?"

"Perfectly acceptable," Jim replied as they sped away from his house. "Now, I'm going to take a stab at this little visit and assume it's not just to celebrate me being taught what I'd spent years doing."

"Close," Gene said as they approached Venice Pizza. "I did want to congratulate you on finishing at the top of your class and also impart some good information."

"Top of my class, my ass," Jim said as they parked. "It's a pass-fail system. No class ranking. Either you proceed to the next level, or you keep trying until the company decides they have wasted enough money on you."

"And since I'd spent almost five years flying the same damn airplane, it wasn't too difficult," he continued as they walked to the front door of the restaurant.

"I guess that means it didn't take too many bananas this time around, then," Gene quipped, referring to Jim's statement about being able to teach a monkey to fly if you had enough bananas.

"Gentlemen," the owner said as he saw them coming in. "It's been quite a while since I've seen the two of you."

"Vacation," Jim said as he led them to a table in the rear.

"I was out of town," Gene said, looking around to ensure they had some privacy.

"I had a flat tire," Jim joked, taking a seat. "The dog ate my map. There was a full moon. I lost my way. I thought there was a closed sign on the door when I drove by."

"Don't pay him any attention," Gene said as he picked up a menu. "He's always been a wiseass. He'll probably die a wiseass. And you should expect it out of him by now."

"I understand," the owner said, smiling. "Regardless, it's good to see both of you again. Two ice teas?"

"Perfect," Jim said, looking up from the menu he had barely glanced at. "Unsweet."

"I'll have them right out," he said, turning away.

"Okay, what's the real reason for your visit?" Jim asked as soon as the waitress had brought their tea and taken their orders.

"First, there's been some unusual activity with Henry's company," Gene answered. "We think he's starting to realize that he has a leak, or maybe starting to realize that he's being fed false information."

"That's not good," Jim said, thinking about the consequences if Henry decided that he wasn't really separated from Black Water. "Anything specific? I'm referring to me."

"No, not yet," Gene told him. "Since there hasn't been any communication between the company and you, he has no reason to think you're still active."

"But Debbie's people have been picking up some strange conversations between Henry and his guy inside Black Water," Gene continued. "Mainly, he's starting to question everything his guy tells him. Keeps asking why so much information has been proven wrong when they've been denied certain contracts or when our people they're looking for are never at the locations he's provided."

"Looks like we need to start accelerating our schedule," Jim said as the waitress entered the room with their meals.

"We're doing just that," Gene told him as soon as she'd left. "And that brings me to you specifically."

"I'm pretty much ready," Jim said taking a fork full of Lasagna and blowing on it. "All I'm waiting for is the IOE."

"That's being taken care of," Gene said. "I've made some suggestions to certain people within the training department at American and have been assured that you'll be placed at the top of their list. I expect you'll get a phone call tomorrow giving you a three-day trip with layovers in Chicago and Denver."

"Again, I'm not surprised," Jim said, shaking his head. "The tentacles of Black Water seem numerous and lengthy."

"We try. We try," Gene said as he sat back and looked at Jim. "Now the question is, when will you be ready?"

"I'll be ready when I get back from Denver if your people have a location for my first adventure," Jim answered as the chance to avenge Jennifer's death was finally within reach. "If you have the necessary items I've requested, just give me a name, a date, the time, and the location. I'll be ready."

Chapter Sixteen

The following morning, as he sat watching the news and having his second cup of coffee, American Airlines Crew Scheduling called advising him they had assigned him a three-day trip for his IOE departing DFW at ten o'clock the next day.

Less than an hour later, Gene called to say that Black Water was initiating the first phase of their program in two days to eradicate Henry's organization, and they'd coordinate with him to ensure there wouldn't be any conflicts with his operations.

Even though all of those of interest to Jim were currently in the Fort Worth area, the company fully expected some, if not all, of them, would be moving elsewhere as Henry became aware of a concerted effort to eliminate many of his operatives.

Gene also told Jim that there would be a car parked next to his truck in the employee parking lot when he got back from Denver. Everything he had requested the company provide would be in the trunk of the car, and the keys would be beneath the rear bumper of his truck.

"We'll let you know before you leave Denver where your people are," Gene told him. "I'm expecting at least one of them to still be in the Fort Worth area. How are you doing regarding your primary interest?"

"I'm taking a little drive this afternoon out to see an old friend," Jim answered. "I've spoken to him about a possible hog hunting trip up north of where he lives. He says there is a shit load of hogs up there tearing up the land around the Bowie and Vashti area."

"Is this old friend a Marine?" Gene asked.

"Nope," Jim told him. "Air Force. And a pilot for American. You might be interested in looking into him as a potential recruit for Muddy Water."

"What's his name?" Gene asked. "I'm interested in him right now because of his potential involvement in one of our operations."

"Butch North," Jim answered. "Has a little ranch about 20 miles north of Fort Worth in Aurora."

"Aurora. Why does that sound familiar?" Gene asked.

"Probably because there was supposedly a UFO that crashed there back in the 1890's," Jim told him. "At least that's the story Butch told me when we were going through one of the annual retraining classes a couple of years ago."

"I'll have Debbie do her stuff," Gene said. "What sort of involvement do you plan for him?"

"Possibly sort of like a Bed and Breakfast for an honored guest," Jim answered. "His place is pretty isolated, and it's difficult for any unannounced visitors to make it up to his house."

"I thought you were going further north of that," Gene said.

"Ultimately," Jim replied. "This'll be sort of a question-and-answer stop for my guest. Which, by the way, is a chance for you to get any information you're interested in."

"I'll get back to you on that," Gene told him. "I really don't know of anything we need from the gentleman. Debbie has pretty much dissected his organization, and I doubt there are any aspects we don't already know. But I'll ask around to see if anyone has any specific questions."

"While you've got Debbie looking into Butch, you might want to add Mike Bitterroot to her search," Jim suggested. "He's the owner of the place up north where we'll be hunting hogs. He should be easy to find. Probably not that many Bitterroot Marines with two tours in Vietnam and a couple of Bronze Stars. Rather reclusive these days."

"Bitterroot?" Gene asked. "Native American?"

"Not sure," Jim answered. "Possibly from the Oklahoma Hacksaw Tribe. Butch may know. They've been friends for several years."

"Hacksaw tribe, anyway I'll have her on it," Gene replied, smiling and shaking his head. "Also, make sure you have your company phone with you and check it before you depart Denver. Once things start, we want to be in constant contact with you. Especially once you get back and we have a definite location for your meeting."

"I was going to leave it in my truck and check it when I got back," Jim told him. "But I'll take it with me and give you a call when I get to the car if you haven't left me any messages."

"One other thing," Gene said. "There's a package beneath the driver's seat that has a driver's license, an FBI badge and ID, a couple of credit cards, and a few other items for a certain Ronald Suggs. If you determine you need anything else, give me a call, and we'll take care of it."

"Definitely," Jim said. "I'll also let you know how it went after my visit this afternoon."

"Sounds good," Gene told him. "I'll be waiting for your call."

Chapter Seventeen

Shortly after hanging up with Gene, Jim called Butch's number and confirmed that he was home. After telling him he would be there within the hour, Jim sat his empty cup in the sink and grabbed the keys to his Corvette.

Checking his map, he decided to take 635, the loop that ran around Dallas, to just north of DFW and join Highway 114, which would take him out to Aurora.

Traffic was fairly light for the time of day, and he was ahead of his self-imposed schedule, so he decided to make a slight change of plans and go north on 121, where he knew there was a Cinnabon bakery. Having discussed how much they both liked them and would look for them at the airports prior to the first flight of the day, Jim decided he'd grab a couple and take them with him.

Although slightly further, he decided to continue north on Farm Road 2491 and go around the top of Grapevine Lake. Then head west on 1171 through Flower Mound toward US I-35W. This more scenic drive wouldn't add more than a few minutes but would avoid all of the traffic on 114 between Grapevine and Butch's place.

As he pulled off 114 on Farm Road 718, he saw that Butch had opened the gate for the driveway that ran a couple of hundred yards down to the low rambling ranch-style house.

Pulling in front of the garage, he had barely shut off the engine when Butch came around the corner wearing his familiar black cowboy hat.

"Hey, Jarhead," Butch called out as he stepped up to the car. "I was afraid I'd have to call in a Forward Air Controller to find you and show you how to get here." "Fat chance," Jim retorted, climbing out of the car and shaking Butch's hand. "You forget Marines are used to grounding navigation while you sissy ass Air Force flyboys need some schmuck with radar to guide you from just outside the target area, where you don't get shot at, back to the Officer's Club. And then you get an Air Medal for being, and I quote, 'Instrumental in the safe evacuation of troops under fire with only minor damage to the forces that had come under great peril and risk of annihilation'. End quote."

"Whatever," Butch said, stepping back and looking at Jim. "What's it been, two, maybe three years?"

"Something like that," Jim agreed. "Too long. How are things out here at the Check Six Ranch? Still roping?"

"Things are good," Butch answered. "Most of my roping is here in my own arena, though. Too much work to get up at three o'clock, load the horses, drive two or three hours and then spend all day just to make a couple of runs at some roping where I don't know a soul. Then drive back. Since most of the guys I used to rope with have moved, died, or decided to sit on their backsides and watch Gunsmoke, it's just not that much fun anymore."

Motioning to the house, Butch said, "Let's go inside where there are chairs, and we don't have to stand around like a couple of heathens. Oh, I forgot, you're a Marine. But let's go inside anyway."

"Hang on just a second," Jim said as he reached inside his car and brought out the box with the Cinnabons. "Thought I'd provide a little something to help contribute to the ever-expanding waistline you've seemed to develop since I last saw you."

"Cinnabons," Butch exclaimed. "I'm going to take back every demeaning word I've ever uttered about the Marines and you in particular. Hell, if you'd just shower more than twice a month, you could almost pass for an officer and a gentleman and be allowed into the hallowed halls of the Air Force Officer's Club.

Glancing in the garage as they headed for the back door, Jim observed, "I see you still have that ratty old Corvette."

"And I see that yours still needs a wash and wax," Butch replied as he opened the door. "But what do you expect from someone who thinks olive drab is actually a color."

Chapter Eighteen

Leading him into the living room, Butch said, "Have a seat, and I'll grab us some coffee. Still take yours black?"

"Always," Jim said, looking around the room. "Better grab yourself a napkin while you're there. I know how you Air Force guys abhor licking your fingers and wiping your hands on your jeans."

"With Cinnabon, I'll lick my fingers until they prune to make damn sure I get every bit of their deliciousness. Not a smidgen gets away from my taste buds," Butch told him, setting a cup of coffee on the low table in front of the couch.

Setting the open box with the Cinnabons on the table, Jim said, "How are the girls? Two, if I remember right."

"They're fine," Butch answered. "Getting bigger and mouthy."

"What would you expect? They *are* your girls," Jim said, taking one of the Cinnabons from the box.

"I guess that's part of the old nature-nurture debate," Butch replied, taking the other one.

"By the way," Butch said solemnly. "I'm sorry to hear about your wife."

"Thanks," Jim answered. "It's still difficult to walk into the house and know that she's not there and won't be coming back."

After pausing for a minute, Butch asked, "So, what do you need me to do? You mentioned something about needing a place to, how did you put it, have a serious private discussion with someone who had been involved with your wife's death?"

Jim sat his coffee down and looked at Butch, saying, "Let's leave it at serious private discussion for right now. And yes, it's because of Jennifer's death. How much do you know about what happened?"

"I heard that she was hit in some drive-by shooting down in Fort Worth," Butch answered. "Knowing how some of the Mexican gangs are down there, I'm surprised there aren't more incidents like that."

"That's not exactly the way it went down," Jim corrected him, leaning forward. "What I'm about to tell you doesn't leave this room. When I'm finished, you can decline any involvement if that's your choice, and I won't think any less of you."

Waiting to see if Jim was going to continue, Butch finally asked, "What really happened?"

"Jennifer and I were down on Exchange Avenue starting a little vacation that was supposed to be an evening there before going to San Antonio to visit some friends," Jim told him. "Just after we had crossed the street to go to the White Elephant, a car pulled beside us, and I heard someone call my name.

I looked and saw gun barrels sticking out of the car's windows," Jim said. "As I was pushing Jennifer to the ground and trying to shield her, all hell broke loose. I was told later how many shots were fired, but I was hit by 20 or so."

Stopping to compose himself, he finally continued, "One of the bullets meant for me struck the sidewalk beneath me and hit her in the side of her head."

"Oh shit," Butch said, comprehending what Jim had gone through. "Did it have anything to do with the gangs down there? And why would they target you?"

"Not the gangs, and I can't go into parts of this right now," Jim answered. "Maybe someday, but for now, let's just say it *was* one of the gangs. It really doesn't matter for our purposes who was responsible other than the man I'm planning on bringing out here. He's responsible because he targeted me, and that was the ultimate reason my wife died. And now he's going to answer for her death."

Butch sat back in his chair and saw the emotion in Jim's eyes, and finally said, "What do you need me to do?"

"First, please don't ask questions about who this man really is or why he targeted me again. I can't tell you that," Jim explained. "Also, don't question who else, if anyone, besides me, is involved. As far as you and Mike, if he agrees to help me, are concerned, I'm taking revenge for Jennifer's death, and that's the end of it.

If during the course of my actions regarding the guy I'm bringing out, you have a change of mind due to any aspect of what I'm going to do, just tell me, and you can walk away at any point, and I'll understand," Jim continued. "I certainly don't expect you to see things the same way I do. This is deeply personal to me, and it can't be as raw of an emotional issue to you. So, if it's something you don't want to be involved with, let me know."

"No, I can't begin to feel how you do right now," Butch told him. "But I can just imagine what I'd do to anyone who hurt, let alone killed, one of my girls. I'd castrate that son of a bitch and roast his balls right in front of his eyes. Then I'd feed them to the hogs. What's the next step?"

"We go see Mike and see if he wants to be involved," Jim answered.

Chapter Nineteen

"We better take my truck," Butch said as they stepped outside. "Some of the roads where we're going are mostly dirt or gravel, and your little 'Vette may get a little dirt…oh hell, how would you know if it did? Let's just take my truck anyway."

"How far is it, an hour?" Jim asked, climbing into the passenger seat of the one ton dually Chevrolet pickup.

"About that," Butch said, backing out of the garage. "So, how much do you want Mike to know?"

"I'll play that by ear," Jim answered. "Tell me more about him. How'd you meet, how well do you know him, that sort of thing."

"We'll start with how we met," Butch said heading west on 114. "The girlfriend of a friend, or ex-friend, introduced us. This was back in about 94 or 95.

We started running the 'ville almost every weekend," Butch continued. "By 'ville, I'm referring to North Side, down where you were shot.

We'd also hit a bar named Cassidy's in the Holiday Inn just off I-35W," he said as they approached Boyd. "That was our Wednesday night hangout. There was a buffet there that really drew a crowd. Mainly what we politely called ladies of generous proportions.

A funny aside, when I was going to college majoring in Animal Husbandry, I took a class in Livestock Judging," Butch told him, laughing as he turned north on FM 730 toward Decatur. "Anyway, the one thing that really stuck in my mind was how to judge pigs. The phrase that stuck with me was 'Walks out wide, front and rear, with three inches of back fat.' That was supposed to be how you described a champion hog.

So, we happened to be down at Cassidy's one night, and there was this rather full-figured lady who elbowed her way past me up to the buffet," he continued. "Anyway, when I left the buffet empty-handed, Mike looked at me, nodded toward the lady, and said, 'Walks out wide, front and rear, with three inches of back fat. Folks, we have a winner.'

Now, having told you that little story, you can safely assume that Mike doesn't care much for plus-size women," Butch said, glancing over. "Matter of fact, he doesn't care much for women, period. Especially those in the military.

Along those same lines, Mike doesn't care for numerous groups," Butch admitted. "Let's just say that the man is best described as an acquired taste. You'll figure that out within ten minutes of talking to him.

On the plus side, the man is loyal to his friends," Butch said as they approached the intersection of 730 and 287. "But his list of friends is most likely in the single digits. It's not because he's not a friendly guy, but he's about as subtle as a sledgehammer. That little filter between your brain and your mouth is completely nonexistent with Mike. A thought passes through where the filter should be and spews forth."

"My biggest question is would you trust him with something like we're planning?" Jim asked.

"I am going to take a wild assed guess and say that this isn't just a hog-hunting trip," Butch said. "I'm thinking there's a tie between bringing your man out to my place and something to do with Mike."

"Possibly," Jim answered. "That depends on your answer as to the level of trust you have in the man."

"I'd put my life in his hands," Butch said seriously. "The man has his faults, more than most people probably. But, some of it's common to a lot of the Vietnam vets. You probably know more about that than I can ever imagine since you spent two tours over there as a mud grunt before you went back in the F-4."

"Yeah, it really did a number on a lot of people," Jim admitted. "People did things that they'd never imagine they'd do after being in country and seeing how inhumane people can be. Sometimes, I feel lucky that most of it really never affected me. Although it did shine a light on how easy it is for one man to kill another."

"Killing people," Butch informed him. "If there's one thing that Mike was good at over there, it was killing. He never fit in once he came back here. Even the Marines wanted to distance themselves from him. But I'll stand by my statement regarding trusting him with my life. Guess I'm one of the single digits he lets into his world."

Chapter Twenty

When they finally arrived at Mike's place, Jim looked around and said, "I thought you said the hogs up here are tearing up all the land. I haven't seen any real damage."

"Mike has been extremely vigilant in trying to keep the hog population down on his property," Butch explained as they drove up the driveway. "Plus, there isn't as much cover for them where the land is kept clear of undergrowth, and they can't hide during the day."

Seeing Mike standing beside an old red pickup, Butch pulled up beside it and said, "Is this the residence of Mad Mike, the number two hog killer of North Texas?"

"I'm not sure about that residence thing, but this is damn sure my place," Mike said, smiling as they got out of Butch's pickup. "And that'd be the number one hog killer to you, Kemosabe.

How are you doing pussy ass flyboy," Mike said, stepping over and hugging Butch.

"Fine as frog hair split three ways," Butch said, extracting himself from Mike. "Mighty fine. Now, I'd like to introduce you to Jim Lashley, the guy I told you about who wants to come hunt hogs."

"Good to meet you, Jim," Mike said, extending his hand. "Welcome."

"Good to meet you, too," Jim said as his hand was enveloped by Mike's. "Thank you for letting me come visit."

Turning to Butch, Mike said, "Okay, why don't one of you tell me why you did come up here. It's damn sure not to hunt."

As Butch looked at Jim, Mike continued, "Come on, guys. Here you are in starched jeans, cowboy boots, and no weapons in the pickup. It doesn't take a rocket scientist to figure it out."

"Guess I'm the reason," Jim answered. "First, I apologize if you were under the impression that we would be going out to hunt today. My main purpose in coming today was to have a look at where you live and talk to you about hunting some of the Russian boars that I've heard are abundant up here."

Mike stood looking at Jim for a couple of minutes and then said, "After Butch told me about you, I did a little research. I had heard about you when I was over there but didn't connect the two. You're the guy who brought those guys down from the hill after you got trapped and were the only one to survive."

"I guess that was me," Jim said, nodding. "But it was nothing that any other Marine wouldn't have done. We don't leave our men behind regardless of their condition."

Again staring at him, Mike finally extended his hand and said, "Welcome, Colonel. I may not have a fancy title for my place like pussy ass here, but as the Mexicans say, mi casa es su casa. Now, what can I do for you?"

"Is there somewhere we can go sit down and have a little talk?" Jim said, looking up at Mike, guessing he was at least six feet and three inches, probably around 250 or 260 pounds. "I'd like to ask you a few questions. And by the way, my name is Jim. There's no Colonel in front of it."

"Sure thing," Mike answered, turning for the house. "I've got a semi-fresh pot of coffee on the stove, a bottle of Jack Daniel's, or some warm milk for our Air Force pussy boy."

"What an asshole," Butch said, following them into the house. "Here I am trapped out in some back woods' version of Deliverance with two semiliterate Mongols wanting to start some, how big is yours contest. Either that, or they're about to have a long-lost lovers reunion, blubbering over each other with man hugs and back-slapping. Neanderthals. Marines are Neanderthals."

"Quiet back there, jet jock," Mike said, leading them into the kitchen. "If we want anything out of you, we'll squeeze it out. How do you like your coffee, Colonel."

"Please, make it, Jim, and black is fine," Jim said, enjoying the interplay between the two guys.

After handing Jim a cup, Mike said, "Have a seat at the table, Butch knows where the milk is and can get his own."

Taking a chair across the table from Jim, he said, "You're on deck. What do you want to talk about?"

Trying to think of the best way to start the conversation, Jim finally said, "I have a little bit of a personal problem that we'll get into later. But let's get into the hog issue first. Are there just feral hogs up here, or are there any Russian boars?"

"Both," Mike answered as Butch joined them at the table. "Actually, there are very few true Russian boars left. They were originally brought over for hunting, mainly on game ranches. They got loose or were turned loose and started breeding with the feral hogs. Now, a feral hog is actually just a domestic hog that has been forced to live in the wild."

"What's the difference between the feral hog and the Russian boar?" Jim asked, taking a sip of his coffee.

"The Russian has a longer snout, bigger head, longer tusks, longer legs, and has a very distinctive hair pattern," Mike explained. "However, if you're looking at a fourth or fifth-generation descendant from the Russian boar, it may not be as pronounced. Are you looking for a specific type of hog?"

"Probably something as close to the Russian boar as possible," Jim answered. "I certainly don't know as much about them as you, but I've heard that they're more aggressive than the feral hog."

Thinking for a second, Mike agreed, saying, "You could say that generally. Again, how far removed from being domestic is the feral hog? How far down the ladder is the Russian? Depends on the individual hog."

Nodding, Jim asked, "Do you think you could find a couple of Russian boars that would be more aggressive than the normal hog?"

"Probably," Mike said with a quizzical look. "What are you really after?"

"One more quick question," Jim told him. "I understand that hogs are omnivorous, is one breed more so than another. What I'm asking is, would the Russian boar be more likely to be carnivorous than a mostly feral hog?"

"Probably the Russian," Mike replied after thinking for a few seconds. "Mainly because he's been forced to live in the wild longer than a domestic that's gone feral. And how hungry is he? Female hogs have been known to eat their young if hungry enough."

"What would be left if a Russian boar was hungry and came across a calf in someone's pasture?" Jim asked.

"He'd probably use his tusks to rip open the underbelly or maybe snap a leg to get it down," Mike answered. "Then he'd tear it apart and devour it. Hell, depending on the size of the hog and of the calf, it's not likely there would be anything left come morning."

Mike suddenly sat back and said, "You're not hunting hogs. You're looking for a place to dispose of something. Or someone."

Chapter Twenty-one

For the next hour, Jim told Mike how Jennifer had died and why he wanted to bring Henry out there. When Mike promised to find a couple of Russian boars that he could trap and make them available when Jim was ready, Jim explained that he had a couple of other things that needed to be resolved first, and it would probably be a couple of weeks before he would be back.

After telling Jim how he would build the cage to hold the hogs and the object of the project, Mike also told them how he would make sure the hogs were always slightly hungry and ensure they had developed a taste for blood.

Satisfied that he could depend on Mike to make all the required preparations, Jim and Butch thanked him and headed back to Aurora.

"What do you think of Mike?" Butch asked as they headed south on 287.

"Different," Jim admitted. "Definitely wound a little tight, but hearing some of his stories about his time in country before he came back to the States sort of explains a lot. There's a lot of pent-up anger there."

"If nothing else, I think you've given him a project he's going to rather enjoy," Butch added. "I'd be willing to bet he's setting up game cameras all over his place and probably most of the neighbors' land right now."

"He reminds me a lot of one of my cousins," Jim said. "Pretty much the same attitude, but seems to contain it better. Mike's pretty vocal about what he thinks."

"You know what frosts my pumpkin?" Butch replied as they saw Decatur come into view. "Some of these people who claim they have Post Traumatic Stress Disorder because they saw a picture of a homeless man. Or heard an off-color story. They have no idea of what PTSD really is."

"I agree," Jim acknowledged. "Reduces the seriousness of the real problem. If Miss Suzie claims she has PTSD because little Johnny showed her his penis on the playground when she was only eight years old and now can't have a relationship with any man, how can anyone compare that to a man who watched his friends' heads explode standing right next to them?"

"I know," Butch agreed. "Or the guy who became so calloused from some of the things he did over there, he becomes unfeeling toward acts of cruelty once he comes home."

"Hell, it wasn't just Vietnam," Jim said as they turned onto 730, heading south out of Decatur. "I remember some of the stories my dad and his World War Two friends told when they didn't know I could hear. Maybe their generation was tougher than ours."

"Not necessarily tougher," Butch countered. "Just willing to take responsibility for their own lives. Instead of whining and blaming others for their issues, they shouldered their problems and moved on. Nowadays, the snowflakes break into tears at the slightest thing that doesn't fit their idea of how life should be. Hell, I can't imagine what most people would think about what you're planning."

"You know, in general, I don't really give a shit what people think of how I live my life," Jim said as they neared Boyd. "I do what I was taught about living an honorable life. Maybe I'm a little harder on other people than most. Hell, I'm probably harder on myself than I am on them. But in this instance, my give-a-shit meter is pegged at zero."

"I'm with you on that," Butch said as they came to his ranch. "Most people have never seen death up close except when a family member dies a natural death at 90. It's not even close to when you're holding someone whose blood is covering your arms and legs. Especially when there was no reason for it to happen, as with your wife. Yeah, the man who started that ball rolling deserves exactly what you're planning. And if you need anything, anything at all, call me."

"I will," Jim promised as they parked at the house. "I'll be back in touch with you when I get a better idea of when the time is right. But I think it might be better if we restricted your involvement to just letting me use your place before I take Mr. Lamance to meet Mike and his pet pig."

"I appreciate your concern," Butch said as they got out of the pickup. "I'm not too worried about it. Most people never know when I'm home, and they're used to seeing other cars or pickups coming to my house. If I'm home when you need to come out, do so. If I'm on a trip, you have the gate code."

"Thanks," Jim replied, shaking his hand. "I'll do my best to let you know as far in advance what my plans are. But, I do appreciate your offer, and also, thank you for introducing me to Mike."

Shaking Jim's hand, Butch smiled and said, "I'd hold off on thanking me about Mike. I love the guy to death, but you've only seen the surface. After years of running with him, I've learned one thing…when you're out in public, be ready for some confrontational situations. As I said earlier, he's an acquired taste."

Chapter Twenty-two

Jim had been back home in Mesquite for less than an hour when Gene called him, asking, "What did you think of Mr. North?"

"Pretty straightforward guy," Jim answered. "What did your research on him show?"

"Positive," Gene told him. "One minor incident regarding hiring someone that some obscure government agency was interested in some years ago. Other than that, good military history, good reputation within his community, excellent reports from American Airlines, nothing derogatory."

"I'd say that's pretty accurate," Jim replied. "Are you considering recruiting him?"

"At this very moment, no," Gene answered. "I'd rather wait to see how he reacts to working with you."

"I'm not going to involve him," Jim said. "At most, I'll use his ranch as a sort of staging point to deal with my problem."

"I thought you were going to start there for the interrogation," Gene responded. "What changed your mind?"

"First, if things go to shit, I don't want to get him involved," Jim explained. "And I think I've found a better scenario that's more conducive to persuading Henry to be more forthright with his answers."

"Before we move on to that, what do you think of North's involvement with our organization?" Gene asked. "Since you are removing him from your plans, what do you think based on your time with him today?"

"I'm going to say no," Jim answered. "I started thinking about it after you said you were going to have Debbie look at him, and I thought you might be interested in him as a prospect. I'm just not sure he has the optimum attitude for our line of work."

"Really?" Gene asked quizzically. "I thought you might have a more favorable opinion. Both of you have similar backgrounds, independent attitudes, and sound like similar personalities. What's the problem?"

"I don't really know how to describe it, maybe more of a lackadaisical attitude," Jim mused. "He just doesn't strike me as being as calloused as this line of work sometimes requires."

"But he's willing to help you with this issue," Gene argued.

"I got the impression that he's supportive of my desire for revenge, just as he would be if it involved one of his children," Jim replied. "Hell, he'd probably sit in the courtroom and cheer if the death penalty was handed down if it involved someone who had harmed someone close to him. But up close and personal? I'm not so sure."

"Okay, that's good enough for me," Gene said.

"Now, on the other hand, I thoroughly believe that the other guy, Bitterroot, would be more than happy to leave a blood splatter across the hotel lobby if he saw someone taking more than one mint from the candy bowl at the front desk," Jim told him. "Let me put it this way; subtle is definitely not his color. If the situation called for a BB gun, he'd go Rambo and pull out his M60E3 mini gun like that guy in Predator used to mow down half the jungle forest in Central America where some cabinet minister's helicopter crashed."

"Isn't that exactly what you're doing?" Gene asked him. "Using a mini gun when a simple 9 mm to the head would do the trick?"

"This is different," Jim countered. "This is personal. The man had my wife killed."

"Technically, he tried to have you killed," Gene reminded him. "Unfortunately, things went wrong."

"I know exactly who he was after," Jim argued. "And if he'd planned or executed a good plan, no one else would have been collateral damage. That's the difference between someone like him and someone like me. If the mission is to remove a single person, I'll wait until I can take care of it without some innocent soup eater at the diner having to die."

"I'm not disagreeing with you," Gene said. "All I'm saying is that you aren't above overkill either. And I do understand it. You know exactly how I cared for Jennifer. Am I going to attempt to change your mind? No. Do I endorse it as a general rule? No. But I agree with your summation regarding hiring someone whose first impulse is to release Armageddon with the slightest provocation. And Debbie's research bears out your feelings. A good man to know about and have as an asset? Yes. To be part of our operation? No."

"Anything else before I get ready for tomorrow's trip?" Jim asked.

"Just one," Gene answered. "You should be ready to take your first adventure when you get back to DFW in three days. We've pretty much isolated the driver, and he's the only one still in the area. I'll have an update when you check in after your trip."

"What's happening on the other issues that were indirectly involved?" Jim asked.

"Let's just say we've started the game," Gene answered. "But it's early in the first quarter, and we're taking our time executing our plays. I plan on coming down to Dallas in a few days, and we can take a look at the game film at that time. Until then, have a safe flight."

Chapter Twenty-three

It was just after noon when Jim landed back at DFW four days later. After telling the Captain that he'd see him next week, he boarded the tram for the parking lot.

As it was rounding the final curve on the north side of the airport, he checked the phone that Gene had insisted he carry with him on the trip. There were still no messages, and he started to wonder if anything had happened regarding his first target.

Hitting the number Gene had programmed into the phone; he finally heard him answer as the tram stopped beside the platform in the parking lot where he had left his pickup.

Getting off the tram, he said, "General, I haven't heard from anyone, so I thought I'd give you a call and see what's developed while I was gone."

"Hang on a second, Jim," Gene told him. "I'm on the line with Debbie."

A couple of minutes later, as Jim was walking to his pickup, Gene came back on the line and said, "We have everything set up for the driver. Are you at the car?"

"Just getting there," Jim answered. "What's the plan?"
"Toss your suitcase in your pickup and get the keys to the car from under your rear bumper," Gene answered. "Let me know when you've got the trunk of the car open."

"Got it," Jim said after locking his suitcase in his pickup. "Looks like a cop uniform and a makeup case."

"Put everything in the front seat of the car and leave the airport through the south exit," Gene directed. "Take 183 when you get there and head west to join 360 South.

You'll be going to the CR Smith Museum, so give me a call when you get there," Gene continued. "Call me back when you find a relatively private spot to park."

Twenty minutes later, Jim had parked at the back of the parking lot as far from any other cars as possible. "Okay, I'm here," he said as Gene answered.

"Good," Gene said. "Now, look in the makeup case. You'll see some wet wipes to clean your face, some yellow-tinted sunglasses, a fairly bushy mustache, a blonde wig, a 9 mm pistol, and an earpiece like you used in El Paso."

"Okay, I've got them," Jim told him as he took everything out and set them on the front passenger seat.

"If there's no one around, take off your American Airlines uniform and put on the police uniform," Gene directed. "Everything should be your size, and there's a Watauga Police ID and an address in the shirt pocket. Call me when you're dressed."

Looking around to make sure no one was watching, Jim opened both doors on the driver's side to shield himself from the view of anyone who may see the car; he began undressing. After putting the cop uniform on, he pulled his black boots back on, slid into the driver's seat, and cleaned his upper lip with the wet wipe. Then, using the rearview mirror to position the false mustache, he pressed it firmly in place and pulled the wig over his hair.

Putting on the sunglasses, he checked himself in the mirror and called Gene. "Okay, I've got everything on," Jim said when he answered. "What's next?"

"The address is for the RZ Sports Bar and Grill in Watauga," Gene answered. "Your man, whose name is Thomas Franklin, should be there in a couple of hours. But first, you need to head for the Walmart that's located a couple of miles west of the bar on North Tarrant Parkway."

"Why am I going to the Walmart when my target is going to be at a bar?" Jim asked.

"He may not be at the bar," Gene explained. "He could be heading there, or he could be leaving there when you arrive. You're going to the Walmart to swap the white Chevrolet for a Watauga Police cruiser that'll be there by the time you arrive.

Now, put the earpiece in, and we'll make sure you have a good connection with the folks that'll be monitoring you and the target," Gene directed. "Stay on the phone until you're talking with them. If you lose connection, call back on this phone. Debbie will be monitoring it to reestablish communication if necessary."

Setting the phone on the dash, Jim slipped the earpiece in his right ear and said, "Hello, anybody listening?"

"I've got you loud and clear," Debbie answered. "How do you hear me?"

"Fine," Jim told her as he started the car. "I'm leaving the museum now, headed west on 183."

"Good," Debbie said. "We'll be monitoring your progress as well as Thomas. Once you get to the Walmart, we should be able to direct you to his location."

Chapter Twenty-four

A few minutes later, Jim was approaching the intersection of 183 and 121 when he heard Debbie telling him to continue west on 121, join 820 westbound, then turn north on 377.

"Where's Thomas?" Jim asked as he maneuvered around some slower traffic approaching the intersection with 820.

"He's still at his apartment," Debbie answered. "His normal pattern is to go to the RZ Grill about half an hour from now. We've followed him there almost every day for the last two weeks."

"Why don't I just go there?" Jim asked, sliding into the right lane to merge with the other cars, trying to leave 121.

"Too many people around his apartment complex," she answered. "We've gamed this several times, and your best chance is to change cars with the police cruiser and head to the RZ. That gives us many more options depending on what Thomas does."

"Okay," Jim conceded, seeing the exit for 377 coming up. "Exactly where will the cruiser be when I get to the Walmart?"

"It just pulled in and is in the reserved spot in front of the store," she told him. "We have a blue Toyota parked next to it that will pull out as you approach."

"And I just get out of this car and get in the cop car?" Jim asked, turning north on 377.

"Of course not," Debbie said sarcastically. "You'll go inside the Walmart and walk through it as if you're a cop headed home looking for some groceries. Then, when you go back out, you'll get into the parked cruiser and leave."

"That sounds good," Jim told her as he crossed Western Center Blvd. "Keys in the cruiser?"

"Yes, and it's unlocked," Debbie informed him. "The guy driving the blue Toyota is there to make sure it wouldn't be disturbed and that you don't have to walk too far passing through the store."

A few minutes later, she said, "You're approaching North Tarrant Parkway. Take the exit and head west. You'll only be about three miles from North Beach Street, where the Walmart is located on your right."

Minutes later, seeing the exit for North Beach Street, Jim made the turn and immediately saw the Walmart. Heading toward the store entrances, he spotted the cruiser with the Watauga Police stenciled on the side.

Making the turn toward it, he saw a blue Toyota just pulling out and blocking another car that was looking to park. Pulling into the open spot, he noticed the driver of the car that was trying to park giving the finger to the driver of the blue Toyota.

Waiting until there weren't any cars near him, Jim exited the car and walked across to the entrance. Nodding to an elderly couple that was leaving, he entered the store and turned right toward the restroom area.

Bypassing the restrooms, he continued to the other exit and left. As he was walking back to where the cruiser was parked, he asked, "Where to now?"

"Thomas hasn't left his apartment yet," Debbie informed him. "The best option right now is to head to the restaurant. If he hasn't left by the time you get there, we'll look at other options."

"Okay," Jim said, getting into the cruiser. "What's the quickest way there?"

"Leave the parking lot, turn left on Beach, left again on North Tarrant for a couple of miles, and take Park Vista Blvd south when you get to it," Debbie answered. "As soon as you turn on Park Vista, look for Sohi Drive on your left. Take it and follow it around the curve for a hundred feet or so. The RZ will be on your left."

"What do you suggest when I get to the restaurant?" Jim asked, turning onto Beach.

"Go ahead and park," she answered. "If you're hungry, go in and grab something to eat. Since Thomas still hasn't left, we're more or less waiting for him to make then next move."

"Okay, I'll head in that direction," Jim told her as he headed east on North Tarrant. "But I'm not going to go in the restaurant and wait. I'll think of something if he isn't moving by the time I get there."

Chapter Twenty-five

As he'd been told, almost as soon as he made the right turn onto Park Vista, he saw Sohi Drive on his left. Making the turn onto Sohi, he was in front of RZ less than a minute later.

Seeing the parking lot almost full, he eased on past and asked, "Any movement?"

"Nope," Debbie answered. "What do you want to do?"

"I'm pulling over on Big View Drive just past the restaurants," Jim told her. "It would look very suspicious if a cop was just sitting in his car in a parking lot. At least here, I could be watching for speeders or someone who didn't stop at a sign. How far is it to where Thomas is?"

"Maybe four miles," she told him.

"Get me over there," Jim said. "If he moves before I get there, give me an intercept."

"Go left on Sohi, and you'll come back to North Tarrant. Make a right. In three or so miles, you'll come to Rufe Snow Drive," she directed. "Make a right on Rufe Snow, and you'll come to Hightower Drive in a couple of miles.

Once you get there, you'll turn left, and you'll be about 500 feet from the apartment complex where he lives," she told him.

"On my way," Jim said, pulling back onto North Tarrant. "What sort of vehicle does he drive?"

"A brown Dodge pickup," Debbie answered.

"He just came out of his apartment," Debbie suddenly exclaimed. "He'll be to his truck in about five minutes."

"I'm turning on Rufe Snow," Jim said. "Give me a cross street between me and his location."

"Straight ahead less than a mile you'll come to North Park Drive," she said. "If you make a right onto it, you can turn around and be facing Rufe Snow if he comes the way we expect."

As Jim pulled into a driveway to turn around after making the right turn, Debbie called, saying, "He's on Hightower, and it looks like he's going to come your way in a couple of minutes. What's your plan?"

"I'm going to light him up as soon as he passes me," Jim answered, pulling to the stop sign. "Where is he now?"

"On Rufe Snow, a little over half a mile south of you," she answered.

Seeing the brown pickup approaching, Jim checked the location of the light switch for the red and blue lights and waited for Thomas to pass in front of him. Seconds later, the brown Dodge crossed North Park, and the driver glanced at him as he passed.

Jim immediately turned on his lights and pulled out behind him. As the brake lights of the truck came on, Jim slowed and waited for him to pull to the curb.

Stopping behind Thomas, Jim sat for a moment as if he were running the truck's tags. Rechecking that his pistol had a round in the chamber, he finally stepped from the car and walked slowly to the driver's door.

As he approached, Thomas said, "Good afternoon, officer. Can I help you?"

"Turn the car off, please," Jim told him.

Waiting until he killed the engine, Jim then said, "Driver's license, please."

"Certainly, sir," Thomas said, reaching for his wallet. "Did I do something wrong?"

Jim accepted the license and confirmed that it was who he was looking for and said, "Could you please turn down the radio?"

As Thomas looked to his right at the radio that was off, Jim pulled his pistol and had it at his temple when he turned back.

"You asked if you did something wrong," Jim said, holding the pistol against his head. "Yes, you did. You're the man who was driving the car that held the men who tried to kill me a year ago. You're the man that drove the car full of men that killed my wife."

Pausing, he said, "Now you're the man that's going to die."

Pulling the trigger, Jim watched the right side of Thomas's head explode and splatter blood across the dash and passenger window. As his body fell forward onto the steering wheel, Jim dropped the gun onto his lap and calmly walked back to the waiting cruiser.

Shutting off the lights, he pulled away from the curb and headed north. As he approached North Tarrant, he told Debbie, "I'm going back to Walmart to get the car and return to DFW for my truck. Tell Gene the gun is in the pickup with the deceased, and I'm going home to take a shower and have a Jack and Coke or three. Let me know when the next man is ready."

Jim was almost home when his phone rang. Answering, he heard Gene asking, "How are you doing?"

"Fine," Jim answered. "Did I leave you with any problems?"

"Nope," Gene answered. "Do you think you'll be ready to go to Chicago tomorrow?"

"I suppose," Jim answered. "What, or who, is there?

"We're running a little operation that parallels yours," Gene told him. "And it just so happens that one of the guys you want is up there working with some of the guys we want. Like to join us?"

"Sounds good to me," Jim said. "Where and what time?"

"The jet will be at Love Field tomorrow morning at nine o'clock, ready to take you to join the others," Gene said. "If everything goes as planned, you'll be home tomorrow night."

"Fine," Jim told him as he turned onto the street where he lived. "I'll be there."

Chapter Twenty-six

The next morning, Jim was already at Love Field when the company Gulfstream III landed and taxied to the General Aviation area located on the north end of the field.

Watching as it pulled to the terminal, he was reminded of the number of times Gene had allowed Jennifer to travel with him when he needed to be in Quantico. How she enjoyed being treated like royalty with *her* private jet.

As the door opened and one of the pilots descended, Jim grabbed his suitcase and headed out to meet him. "Good morning," Jim said as he got to the airplane. "I'm Jim Lashley. Guess I'm going with you to Chicago."

"Good morning, Jim," the pilot said, shaking Jim's hand. "I'm William Jackson, the copilot. The Captain is Peter Frost. Just leave your bag by the stairs, and I'll bring it on board for you."

"That's not necessary," Jim said. "I'll take it up and toss it on one of the seats if that's okay. Do you know if there are any other people going with us?"

"Should be three more," William answered. "But they aren't due here until nine."

"Is it all right if I go on up?" Jim asked, wondering if the other passengers were part of the team he would be working with.

"Sure," William told him. "I'm doing a quick walk around while we're waiting for the fuel truck. Just introduce yourself to Peter. He'll probably be coming out in a few minutes to check the weather in Chicago, but he's talking to the company about a stop-off in Oklahoma City to pick up another passenger."

"Okay, thanks," Jim replied, grabbing his suitcase. "I'll check in with him when he's not busy."

Jim was setting his suitcase in the seat across the aisle from where he wanted to sit when Peter stepped out of the cockpit. "Good morning," Jim said, turning to greet him. "Jim Lashley."

"Hello, Jim," Peter said, shaking his hand. "Peter Frost. Most people call me Jack."

"That's understandable," Jim said, looking at the mass of white hair and beard. "Which do you prefer?"

"I'll answer to either, but Jack seems to the preference of everyone else," he said smiling.

"Jack, it is then," Jim replied. "Any seat here, okay?"

"Sure," he told him. "Plenty of open seats. Take your pick."

"William said we may be stopping in Oak City for someone," Jim remarked.

"Yeah, some FBI guy the company agreed to ferry back to his office in Chicago," Jack confirmed. "Shouldn't add much time to the trip. Maybe 30 minutes."

"No problem," Jim said as they saw three guys coming out of the terminal.

"Oh, before I forget," Jack said, turning back to the front of the airplane. "I've got an envelope in the cockpit for you. Hang on, and I'll grab it."

He returned a moment later as the three new passengers were climbing the stairs. Handing the envelope to Jim, he turned to the new arrivals and said, "Welcome, gentlemen. I'm Peter Frost, and I'll be flying us to Chicago via Oklahoma City. Grab any open seat, and William will be back in a few minutes to brief you."

After introducing himself to the others, Jim took his seat and opened the envelope. Looking at a picture of a man who looked to be in his mid-40s, he quickly read his biography describing his connection with Henry's organization.

Another rather grainy picture showed the same man sitting in the front passenger seat of a white car and the barrel of a gun visible sticking out of the window. In the background, Jim could make out the front of the Stockyards Hotel.

Finally, he came to a couple of sheets describing who he would be meeting and a basic description of their operation. A list of items he would be provided upon arrival was minimal, basically another earpiece for communications and a 9 mm pistol.

He quickly learned that the three other men on the flight were going to be part of the team Black Water was sending to Chicago for the men they were interested in. Seeing the name of the leader, he rose from his seat and stepped to the rear of the plane, where the man had taken a seat.

"Randy?" Jim said, approaching him. "Could I have a minute?"

"Sure," he answered, motioning for him to take the seat across a small table from his seat.

"I'm not sure how much the company has told you, but I'm supposed to join your team in Chicago," Jim said, handing him the sheet naming the team members.

"We were briefed there would be someone joining us," Randy said, glancing at the sheet Jim had provided. "But we were told that he, meaning you, would only take part at the initial stage and would continue with your part once we had our men."

"That's true," Jim said, nodding. "The company only provided me with the basics. We're to approach the targets at a restaurant where they'll be having lunch, and I'm to remain with one of them while you escort the others, three from what I've read, out of the restaurant."

"That's the basics," Randy confirmed. "We'll have a van and driver waiting at the airport that'll take us to the location, and we'll escort our guys out of the restaurant. We weren't briefed on what you would be doing once we left."

"That's pretty much all I know," Jim said, nodding. "I guess the company will give me a little more guidance when we get to Chicago. Do you know if anyone else is involved?"

"Some guy who's posing as an FBI agent will be accompanying us," Randy said. "He may be the driver. Guess I'll find out when we get there."

"I'll bet he's the reason we're stopping in Oklahoma City," Jim mused. "The Captain told me we were picking up an FBI agent there."

"Probably," Randy agreed. "That would make sense. Maybe he'll have more information about your part of the operation. He wasn't mentioned as going with us after we picked up our guys. I was led to believe that he's just there to provide some 'authenticity' to our operation."

"Gentlemen," Peter said as he entered the airplane. "We've refueled, everyone is on board, and if there's no objection, we'll depart a few minutes early."

As everyone nodded, he continued, "Great. If you'll pay attention to William for his excuse of a flight brief, I'll have us on the way momentarily. If there's anything we can do during the flight, please don't hesitate to give us a call."

Chapter Twenty-seven

As they taxied to the General Aviation terminal at Oklahoma City after landing, Jim saw a single man wearing a simple dark suit leave the building and walk to where the ground personnel were marshaling the Gulfstream.

Leaving the engines running, William left the cockpit and came back to lower the stairs. As the man came in, William turned to the cabin and said, "Gentlemen, this is Rob Sproc. He'll be traveling with us to Chicago."

Rob simply nodded as he made his way back to an open seat. William closed the door and returned to the cockpit. Nothing was said during the taxi back to the runway as everyone waited to see if Rob would make contact.

When Rob leaned his seat back after takeoff and appeared to sleep, Jim glanced at Randy and shrugged his shoulders. Finally deciding that he'd been wrong about their new passenger, Jim leaned his seat back and tried to nap.

After landing at Chicago's Midway airport and taxing to park, they were met by a silver Ford van on the right side of the airplane. As William was opening the stair door for them to get out, he told Jim to leave his bag since they would wait to take him back to Love Field.

Once they had deplaned and were walking to the van, Rob came down and headed toward the terminal, where he was met by a tall brunette who threw her arms around his neck as he approached the terminal door.

"Welcome, gentlemen," the driver of the van said as he slid open the side door. "I'm Kevin Roberts. I was a little worried that you'd be late when I learned about a stop to pick up some FBI guy in Oklahoma.

Anyway, you're actually a little early," he continued as he looked at each of them. "You guys grab a seat, and we'll head to the restaurant. There are backpacks for each of you on the seats. Just find the one with your name and take a peek. If you have any questions, feel free to ask."

Jim slid into the rear seat as Randy joined Kevin in the front. As he was passed his backpack, he found a 9 mm pistol, an extra clip, a box containing his earpiece, and a map of Chicago with a route back to Midway highlighted in yellow.

"If you guys will please take out your earpieces, I'm going to try to establish communications with the lady at Quantico," Kevin said as they pulled out of the airport. "I've checked them once before, but I want to make sure we can all hear and talk to each other before the serious shit starts."

Once everyone had their earpieces in, he continued, "This is Kevin; please check in with your first names."

As everyone said their name to make sure they could both transmit and receive, Kevin used his phone to call Debbie at Quantico.

"Debbie, this is Kevin," he said as they left the airport, heading north on 50. "I've got everyone, and we're heading to Aurora for the meeting."

"Good afternoon, gentlemen," she said. "If you could please give me a voice check."

After hearing everyone, she continued, "The party you're meeting is about 30 minutes from La Quebrada, the restaurant where we heard them plan to meet."

"They're arriving in two cars," she informed them. "The three men the company is interested in are in a tan Honda, license plate 327 NFR. The other man is driving a blue Mazda, license plate 187 PBR."

"Jim, you'll take the Mazda when you leave. The keys will probably be in his pocket," she said. "I'll have one of our people tell you where to go to drop it off when you leave the restaurant. Randy, once you have your guests settled, please have one of your guys follow you in the Honda."

"Are there any questions at this point?" Debbie asked as Kevin joined US 55 heading southwest.

Hearing nothing, she said, "Very well. I'll keep you updated on the location of the other party, but it looks like you'll get there about the time their meals are being served."

"Kevin, we just heard there's an accident on 43 that's backing up traffic," Debbie informed him. "I recommend taking 55 down to 294, then north to 34. After that, join 88 west to 25. The restaurant is on the east side of the Fox River about four miles south of 88."

"Got it," Kevin thanked her. "Let me know if anything else pops up. Chicago traffic can go from crap to crappier at the snap of your fingers."

Chapter Twenty-eight

Pulling into La Quebrada, they spotted the Honda and the Mazda sitting together at the end of the parking lot.

"Anything new?" Kevin asked as they got out of the van.

"No," Debbie answered. "They're sitting at a table near the back wall to the left as you go in. Jim's man is sitting with his back to the wall on the left as you approach and will have the best look at you as you walk toward their table. I'd suggest that Jim hang back so he won't see him first."

"Sounds good," Kevin agreed. "Anything else? Do you know if they have guns?"

"Not that I know of," Debbie told him. "This is just a get-together to discuss an operation. If they had weapons, they probably left them in their cars. My recommendation is not to show yours unless necessary."

"I'm going to assume they're carrying anyway. Everybody ready?" Kevin asked, looking at each man. "I'll lead since I'm the FBI with the badge. Randy, why don't you be behind me and step to my right when I get to the table."

"You other two should come up on my left to keep Jim hidden until the last second," he said again, looking into each man's eyes to make sure they knew where they were expected to be. "Jim, I'd suggest you slide past them on the left once I have their attention."

"All right, let's all check our weapons," Kevin said, pulling his pistol from the holster on his right hip beneath his jacket. "Make sure you have a live round in the chamber in case this goes to hell in a handbasket. And take the guys against the wall first if it comes to that.

The other two will have their backs to us, and it'll be difficult for them to draw, turn, and shoot before we can," he explained. "Also, you two on the left, keep your eyes on them since you can see their eyes. Any questions?"

After everyone nodded and replaced their pistols, Kevin said, "Let's go join the party."

Entering the restaurant, Kevin turned left and spotted the four men where Debbie had said they would be. Walking straight toward them, he looked for any sign of recognition or awareness that he was headed to their table.

Stopping behind the men with their backs to him, he pulled his badge from his pocket and said, "Gentlemen, please remain seated with your hands on the table where I can see them. I'm FBI Agent Roberts, and these agents are here to make sure you don't do anything stupid."

As the two men went left to stand at the end of the table, as Kevin had said, he continued, "So far, this is just a cordial discussion to get some information we believe you possess."

As the men at the table were paying attention to Kevin, Jim slipped to the left and was standing beside his target. Putting his right hand behind his back, he pulled his pistol from the back of his pants and stood with it still hidden.

"Who drove the blue Mazda?" Kevin asked, looking across the table. "License number 187 PBR."

"I did," Jim's target answered, raising his hand slightly. "What did I do wrong?"

"Did you come here by yourself, or did one of these guys come with you?" Kevin asked, looking directly at him.

"I came by myself," he finally said.

"What's your name?" Kevin asked.

"Sam Thompson," he answered.

"Okay, that must mean the other three of you came in the Honda," Kevin told them. "You're the men we want to talk to. Now, if you'd be so polite as to slide your chairs back while keeping your hands in sight, we can step outside and discuss the situation.

You, Sam, will remain seated with your hands on the table until I escort these gentlemen out," he said, looking at him. "The gentleman to your right will remain with you until we return to ensure that you don't go stupid on me. Understand?

However, I must warn all of you that any abnormal movement will have serious consequences," Kevin said, taking a step back. "And by serious consequences, I'm referring to the fact that these gentlemen are armed and rather good at close quarters such as this."

"Gentlemen, on three, slide your chairs back but remain seated until I tell you to rise," Kevin ordered. "Ready? One…Two…Three."

As the men did as they had been told, Kevin then said, "Well done. Now, on the count of three, you will rise and keep your hands visible in front of you. I see no need to remind you of what will happen if you don't. You don't seem to be stupid or foolish, so let's try to keep it that way.

Once you're standing, you in the back by Sam, you'll come around the table, and the gentleman to my right will step back, allowing you to pass him," Kevin explained.

"He'll then follow you outside and wait for the rest of us to join you.

Now, your last two, I'll step back, and you'll stand, turn to your left, and follow your friend," he continued. "The men to your left will be right behind you until we're together again, to quote an old country song, outside.

Let's do this right, folks. There won't be any second chances. Ready? One…. Two…. Three." Kevin counted, taking another step back.

"Very good," he said, watching the men following his directions. "This is going so very well. Now, keep walking, and we'll all make it through this."

As they were leaving, Jim looked down at Sam and said, "Please put your car keys on the table."

"Why?" he asked.

"Because I told you to," Jim said, staring at him. "Do it now."

As Sam pulled the keys from his pocket and placed them on the table, Jim said, "When Kevin asked who drove the blue Mazda, you asked what you did wrong."

"Since he didn't answer your question, I'll do it," Jim said, taking his pistol from behind his back and pressing the barrel against Sam's temple. "You killed my wife."

When Sam's eyes widened with recognition, Jim smiled at him and pulled the trigger. Calmly laying the gun on the table beside Sam's head that had fallen forward, he picked up the keys and strode to the exit.

Once outside, he nodded to Kevin and the others as he passed them on his way to the Mazda. Keying his microphone as he started the car, he asked, "Debbie, I'm heading back to Midway. What would you like for me to do with the car?"

"Just follow the map and take it to long-term parking," she answered. "Let me know if you're having any problems, and I'll get with you. Right now, I need to pay attention to some live problems."

Chapter Twenty-nine

Jim was headed home from Love Field when his company phone rang. Assuming it was Gene, he answered, "Good afternoon, General."

"So it seems," Gene replied. "It's amazing how much a single gunshot can accomplish."

"It accomplished its goal," Jim told him.

"That's not what I'm referring to," Gene said. "When Kevin and the rest of them heard the shot and then saw you calmly walking out with just a nod, the other three suddenly became more cooperative than we ever expected."

"Well, I'm glad there were extra benefits," Jim said as he came into Mesquite. "I guess you know by now that I've left the gun I use at each location. I hope that's not going to cause any problems."

"Not a problem at all," Gene assured him. "I had that covered from the get-go in the event you did it. I figured you wouldn't want to be caught with the gun or even a slight chance of it happening, so I made arrangements to have a cleanup crew standing by to make sure nothing led back to you or the company."

"Do you happen to remember a certain lady named Jewell?" Gene then asked. "Of course you do. Well, she just happened to be a temporary waitress at La Quebrada for the sole purpose of covering everyone's tracks."

"So she's back with the company?" Jim asked, pulling into his driveway. "That's good."

"Yeah, she's back," Gene confirmed. "Still on a somewhat limited scope because she's still having physical issues from the crash, but she's determined to come back full-time. Sort of hard-headed like someone else I know."

"I haven't a clue who you're referring to," Jim said, taking his bag from his pickup. "But I'm sure you didn't call me just to discuss this last operation. What else is on your mind?"

"Sometimes your perceptiveness amazes even me," Gene responded. "To the point, we're looking at setting up another operation that encompasses some aspects of what took place in Chicago."

"As you know, we've been tracking several individuals of interest in addition to the men you're interested in," Gene continued. "We still believe that Henry is becoming suspicious of his mole up here, so we've got a limited window of opportunity to get one more use out of him before we need to remove him."

"What's your plan?" Jim asked, setting his suitcase down as he walked through the living room.

"Letting Henry know we're bringing you back into the company," Gene answered. "It does carry a certain amount of risk for you. Once he knows you're active again, you'll probably become a target."

"How do you think this will benefit Black Water?" Jim asked walking into the kitchen and taking a bottle of Jack Daniel's from the cabinet.

"Twofold," Gene answered. "First, if his goal is still to remove as many of our agents as possible, he'll come after you again since he determined you were an obstacle to his company before. That probably hasn't changed. And, since he's had difficulty in removing any other *obstacles*, we think he'll make a move for you."

"What's the second *fold,* as you put it?" Jim asked, adding Coke to the half-full glass of Jack Daniel's he had poured.

"We think it'll bring in more of his people," Gene said. "Possibly some we aren't aware of at this time."

"So you're asking me to become a target, as I was when Jennifer was killed," Jim told him, taking a sip. "And from what you just said, you fully expect some as of now unknown actors to be involved."

"Meaning I'll be more exposed and in jeopardy than the first time," Jim argued as he stepped out of the back door. "I can somewhat see the benefit to Black Water. What's the benefit to me?"

"Let's do a cost-benefit analysis for me right quick," Jim said, taking a seat at the wrought iron table on the back porch. "Potential cost? I lose. I die. Potential benefit? I don't see one. 'Splain it to me, Lucy."

"Let me ask you this," Gene replied. "What's the cost of your endeavor to take out the men responsible for Jennifer's death? You could definitely lose. Even if it's a minor risk, it's there.

Now, what's the benefit?" he continued. "I'll argue none."

Pausing, he explained, "Just what have you gained from killing two people as of now? What will you gain from the next three? Again, I'll argue none.

Will it bring her back?" Gene asked, dropping his voice. "No. Nothing will bring her back. Don't get me wrong, Jim. I'll stand by your decision if you decide the risk is too great and just want to pursue your vendetta, which is truly what you're doing. Or I'll take every measure possible to keep you safe if you decide to do this.

We have, through the NSA and Debbie, developed an almost instantaneous program to discover any new assets of Henry's company," Gene revealed. "You saw the genesis in El Paso, and now it's expanded exponentially as demonstrated today in Chicago."

Again pausing, he continued, "You know how much you mean to me. It broke my heart when Jennifer left us. To think how I'd feel if the same happened to you is almost unbearable. That would be like losing my family."

"General, you know I'll never turn down any request from you," Jim said, leaning back in his chair. "You've been like a father to me. If not for you, I have no idea where I'd be today. If you hadn't gotten me into the MARCAD program to become an officer and ultimately a pilot for the airlines, as well as that being how I met Jennifer, I'd probably be sitting on a street corner in Seattle holding a cardboard sign asking for people to help a poor homeless vet.

I swore an oath to defend this country over twenty years ago," he continued. "As far as I'm concerned, that oath still stands. And when you ask me to do something that you see as a threat, I'll follow you just as I did when I was in the Corps. What do you need me to do?"

Chapter Thirty

Jim had barely crawled out of bed when he heard the phone ringing from where he had left it in the kitchen last night.

Trudging in to answer it in just his tightie whities, he glanced at the number calling and answered, "Good morning, General. If you'd have waited another ten minutes, I might have had a cup of coffee."

"My apologies," Gene replied. "But I think this will give you the same result as an entire pot of coffee. Less than an hour ago, we intercepted a message from one of the guys we're tracking, and they're having a planning meeting in Denton this morning."

"And that's of concern to me because?" Jim said, dumping the old grounds from the filter of his coffee pot.

"Because the planning is regarding you," Gene informed him. "We picked up the conversation listening to a target we've been planning on interviewing when we heard your name. Debbie's folks tagged the phone immediately."

"That person was an unknown," Gene continued. "But, as we began monitoring his activities, he had a conversation with one of the guys involved in your shooting."

"When the guy we were monitoring was called by the shooter asking when they planned on correcting *a screw-up*, as he put it, he asked to be involved because he wanted a chance to redeem himself," Gene concluded.

"So, do you know the plan?" Jim asked, adding water to the pot.

"No," Gene answered. "We only know that the three men are meeting presumably to do exactly that. Develop a plan. Our hope is to stop them in the preplanning phase. I also thought you might want to be involved since one of the planners is of interest to you."

"So, what is our plan?" Jim asked.

"I have two men who can be at your house within thirty minutes," Gene said. "We know what cars the targets will be driving, we know where they're meeting, and we know when. My only question is, do you want in?"

"I can be ready in ten minutes," Jim said, turning off the still perking pot. "Could you have one of the guys come stop somewhere and grab me a cup of coffee? Possibly from Cinnabon? There's one on Town East Blvd just off Gus Thomasson Road."

"I'll have one of them swing by on his way to pick you up," Gene told him. "Anything else you need?"

"A clean gun and a clear shot," Jim answered, heading back to his bedroom.

"The guy coming to get you already has that, as well as a new earpiece for you," Gene told him. "And he'll be there in ten minutes from now. I'd suggest you put on something other than just your underwear unless you want to be noticed."

"I'll be dressed and waiting out front," Jim said, pulling on a pair of jeans. "I suppose the guy will brief me on the way to Denton."

"That he will," Gene replied. "Now, if you don't have anything else to discuss, I'll start getting the latest information on these guys and see what we can do to stop them from completing exactly what we were discussing last night."

Jim finished dressing and had barely closed and locked his door when a black Suburban with a dark tint pulled to the curb in front of the house.

Opening the door and sliding into the front passenger seat, he said, "Good morning. I appreciate you stopping for some coffee."

"Not a problem," the driver said, accelerating down the street. I'm Jerry."

"Good to meet you, Jerry," Jim said, pulling the top off the coffee cup. "How much can you tell me about what the plan is?"

"A lot of it is playing it by ear," Jerry answered, heading north to join 635. "This is one of those rushed operations where we get minimal information and are expected to get maximum results. We've been promised more details as we get closer."

"I just got off the phone with General Barker, and he's busy trying to do just that," Jim told him. "He also said you had a weapon and an earpiece for me."

"In the glove compartment," Jerry answered as he accelerated well above the posted speed limit.

"Do you know where we're meeting the targets?" Jim asked, taking the only Cinnabon from the container.

"Not exactly," he said as they headed around the north side of Dallas. "I'm meeting Stan, the other guy, at the Golden Triangle Mall in Denton. That's the general area where they're supposed to be. Hopefully, we'll get a better grasp of exactly where by the time we get there."

"Where are the targets coming from?" Jim asked as the sign for the I-35 E exit appeared ahead."

"Don't know," Jerry answered. "All I know is that this came down as a priority mission and we'd be briefed enroute. Other than that, we're flying by the seat of our pants."

"That's a big ass Mall," Jim said as Jerry merged with the northbound traffic on I-35 E. "But the guys back at Quantico can narrow it down to a gnat's ass."

Chapter Thirty-one

"You need to put your earpiece in if you want to listen to what the company has to say," Jerry said as they were passing Lewisville. "They're on the line with an update."

"Can everyone hear me?" a female voice said. Hearing all three of them check in, she continued, "This is Mary. Debbie is working on getting the geosynchronous satellite to focus on the Golden Triangle Mall so we can get you to where the targets will be."

"The first car with two of them has already arrived," Mary continued. "They parked just off San Jacinto Blvd on the north side of the mall parking lot. The other car is still about five miles away, coming up I-35 W. We're just waiting to see if he goes to the first car or if they move elsewhere."

"To keep things simple, I'm going to refer to the first car's occupants as A, the driver, and B, the guy in the front passenger seat," Mary explained. "The last guy in the other car will be C. He's the man Mr. Lashley is coming to meet."

"I'm expecting C to come to where A and B are since they have told him where they're parked," she said. "If that's what's going to happen, you need to take the exit for San

Jacinto and 288. Go beneath 288 and enter the mall parking lot just before San Jacinto. It'll be the second entrance."

"Jerry, since C will beat you to the mall, I suggest you make a slight left and an almost immediate right to head toward the mall when you get there," Mary directed. "Find a parking space anywhere along there and wait until we make sure they're not going to move. Any questions?"

"How crowded is the parking lot?" Jim asked, thinking about how to approach the two cars.

"Unsure," she answered. "We'll know more once the satellite is in the correct position. However, we're expecting it to be relatively empty this early."

"Stan, where are you?" Jerry asked as they crossed the Lewisville Lake bridge.

"I'm almost to the mall," he replied.

"Go ahead and take the exit we were talking about and make a swing around so you can see where they say A and B are parked," Jerry told him. "Let me know what you think."

"No problem," Stan told him. "I should be there in a couple of minutes."

"C is now on I-35 E coming south," Mary told them. "He'll be taking the exit for 288 right behind you, Stan. I'd recommend that you take the first entrance into the parking lot and wait for Jerry. If you make a slight left and park in the first spot you come to, you should have a good view of both cars if they park where A and B are."

"I'm taking the exit now," Stan said. "I'm less than a mile from the mall."

"C is about a minute behind you," Mary advised. "Jerry, you and Jim are about six minutes behind them."

"Good morning, gentlemen," Debbie said, joining the conversation. "I've finally got the satellite looking at the mall, and there aren't very many cars parked there. Especially back where Mary told you the first car is parked."

"They'll be the only cars within 200 feet of any other car," she told them. "Could be a difficult approach if you're trying to be unnoticed."

"Is there a way we can come at them from different directions?" Jim asked.

"I'm in the parking lot," Stan said. "I'm sitting beside a Wendy's, and I can see a single car where Mary said it would be."

"Jerry, if you take the exit we were talking about and go to San Jacinto and turn right, you'll come to another entrance in about a thousand feet down," Debbie said. "If you take that exit and turn right as you enter the parking lot, you'll be facing where the two cars should be."

"I just saw a car enter and head to where A and B are parked," Stan reported. "Okay, he's parking beside them."

"I see them," Debbie said. "Now, C is getting into the back seat of their car. Jerry, you and Jim are about three minutes away."

"Understood," Jerry said seeing the exit sign for San Jacinto and 288. "Jim, what do you suggest?"

"Stan, hold your position," Jim said, mentally working out the approach knowing it was going to be completely in the open. "We'll take Debbie's directions and come at them from the entrance off San Jacinto.

Debbie, what's the approximate distance from where Stan is from their cars and from where we'll enter to get to their cars?" Jim asked as Jerry took the exit.

"About the same distance for both of you," she answered. "Probably about a thousand feet each."

"Stan, can you see the entrance she's talking about on San Jacinto?" Jim asked as they crossed under 288.

"No, the building is in the way," he answered. "I can see San Jacinto but not the entrance."

"No problem," Jim said as they passed the first entrance. "We're just passing where you said you were. You should see us make the turn on San Jacinto since we're the only car on this road."

"I see you," Stan said.

"Do you have a clear path to their car?" Jim asked as they turned right.

"I can drive straight across the lot to them," he answered.

"Okay, get ready to haul ass across to them," Jim told him. "I want you to stop with your car as close to the front bumper of the car they're in as possible. We'll take the rear."

"What then?" Jerry asked. "Neither of us can get out with our doors blocked by their car."

"I'll get out and approach them," Jim said, making sure he had a round in the chamber. "You two just stay in the cars with your guns ready if any of them try to get out of their car. Make sure they can see you pointing your weapons in their direction."

"Go now, Stan," Jim ordered as they turned into the parking lot.

As they accelerated toward the two parked cars, Jim saw Stan barreling down on them also. As Jerry slammed on the brakes, he slid to a stop, slamming into the rear of the car with the side of his.

Jumping from the car, he saw Stan stop inches from the car with his pistol sticking out of the window, pointing at the driver.

Walking around the back of his car, Jim walked unnoticed to the left side of where their targets' car was now trapped. Stepping up to the driver's window, he tapped the glass with his pistol and motioned for him to roll down the window.

"Good morning, gentlemen," Jim said, looking from man to man. "Here for a little early morning shopping?

What I need for each of you to do now is put your hands where I can see them," he continued. "You, driver, put your hand on the steering wheel. You, in the passenger seat, put your hands on the dash. And finally, you in the backseat, raise your right hand and roll down the window with your left."

Once the window was down, Jim said, "Now, raise your left hand and keep both of them up until I say to drop them."

Without another word, he swung his pistol to the driver's window and placed two quick shots to the heads of both men. Then, pointing it in the rear window, he said, "So, you wanted a second chance at me. What did you plan to do this time? Kill another innocent bystander like you did, my wife?"

Jim paused for barely a second and pulled the trigger, saying, "Sorry. No second chances."

Tossing the gun into the rear seat, he walked to Stan's car, climbed into the passenger seat, and said, "I need a ride home since Jerry's car seems to have a little damage. Do you think you can manage?"

Chapter Thirty-two

Jim was doing laundry and repacking his bag for his upcoming trip when the doorbell rang. Pushing the final button to start the dryer, he headed through the house to the front door.

As he opened the door and saw Gene, he said, "General, good morning. Please, come in. Coffee?"

"Coffee would be good," Gene said, stepping into the living room. "Is today a casual workday? I see you're lounging around in sweatpants. I didn't know you owned such things."

"Housework," Jim said, leading them to the kitchen. "I see no reason to get outside dressed when I'm staying inside. This is sort of my Big Lebowski look."

"You're well on the road to pajamas and slippers shopping at Walmart," Gene told him, shaking his head and taking a seat at the table. "Hell, you'll probably let your hair grow and have curlers."

"Nix on the curlers," Jim said, setting a cup in front of Gene. "Maybe a bathrobe to complete the ensemble."

"I guess you'll want me to start calling you *the dude*," Gene joked, taking his cup.

Jim took his cup from the sink and refilled it. Sitting down across the table from Gene, he said, "Only if you grow a big mustache, get a cowboy hat, and drink sarsaparilla. Now, I'm pretty sure you didn't come all this way for a cup of my weak-ass coffee, so what can I do for you?"

Tilting his head slightly, Gene asked, "Do you know the shit storm you started with your little *execution* yesterday?"

"I guess not," Jim answered. "But I'd imagine that Henry Lamance is pretty pissed."

"That's putting it mildly," Gene said. "We had several operations that have had to be changed because he believes he has someone within his organization that's conspiring with us."

"Is that really unexpected?" Jim asked. "And didn't you say that you were going to remove anyone directly involved with the planning or execution of our people?"

"Yes, I did," Gene argued. "But I hadn't planned on you taking out four in two days, along with the ones you weren't involved with. Let's just say Henry lost almost a dozen of his best operatives in less than a week."

"I guess he's getting the message," Jim said, nodding his head. "So, we've accelerated the learning curve. I think it was inevitable that he figured out someone, probably Black Water, was removing his people.

And, regarding yesterday, you were the one who sent me there," Jim continued. "And you knew what I would do when I confronted one of the guys involved with Jennifer's death.

As to the other two, they were a threat to me," Jim said as he sat back. "And I could argue that they were only a threat because the company decided to resurrect me. That places the blame on the company for putting me in a position where I had to confront the threat.

The other two were probably going to be either taken or removed by Stan and Jerry anyway," Jim added after a slight pause. "True?"

"That's correct," Gene answered. "But I was hoping to bring them in and possibly get more information on other agents working for Henry."

"Were they armed yesterday?" Jim asked.

"Of course," Gene said. "We pretty much knew that because there was very little reason for the meeting unless they were coming after you yesterday."

"Another point in my, *they were a threat,* opinion," Jim agreed, nodding. "So, we have these guys getting ready to come after me. Add two good men who are being put in harm's way because of me. And a situation where there is no well-developed plan and little intelligence other than where they were going to be.

I didn't see too many options for me," Jim continued. "Get into a gun battle in the middle of the parking lot at the mall where one or more of us, and possibly some innocent shoppers, are caught in the crossfire? All because of me?"

Shaking his head, he solemnly said, "I couldn't protect my own wife when these people came after me last time. I'll be damned if I'll put more innocent people in jeopardy.

And the 'shit storm' that resulted wasn't just because of this single incident," he added. "It was an accumulation of several actions of the company along with mine. And, as I previously mentioned, it was inevitable sooner or later. It only accelerated the process."

Pausing, he concluded, "Now, General, if you had been in my position, what would you have done?"

Looking at Jim for a few seconds, he finally answered, "I guess I'd have shot the sons-of-bitches in the face. Now, if you'll put on some *outside clothes*, as you put it, I'll take us to lunch."

Chapter Thirty-three

After deciding on Mexican food, Jim changed into his typical long-sleeved white button-down collar shirt, starched Wrangler jeans, and Tony Lama boots. Almost an afterthought, he clipped his Smith and Wesson 45 caliber pistol on his belt.

Walking into the living room, where Gene was looking at an old saddle on a stand made from horseshoes, he said, "Let's head to Forney. There's a place there called Christina's Fine Mexican Restaurant, and I'll guarantee you that there isn't a finer place for Mexican food for at least 20 miles."

"Really," Gene replied, heading for the door. "And what will the other restaurant be?"

"Another Christina's," Jim said, smiling. "Then there's another one 30 miles, another maybe 40 miles, and then…"

"I get the picture," Gene said, laughing. "Are they all so dangerous that you need to carry a gun? Or does this Forney place have a reputation for gunplay?"

"They have a reputation for an excellent Carne Asada with Shrimp Relleno," Jim answered. "The pistol is because your little speech has made me wonder what Henry is going to do regarding Black Water removing so many of his men. If he's getting desperate enough to come after me twice, I think I'd rather have a chance to fight back.

Besides, this is Texas," he continued as they got in Gene's black Suburban. "If you get out of Dallas, I bet you'd be surprised at the number of guys carrying a pistol."

"I thought it was only legal to carry concealed," Gene said, getting into the car. "So, how would you know?"

"Concealed is a vague term," Jim answered. "If I pulled my shirt tail out, I'd be concealing the gun. But I'll just leave it in the car when we go in.

Now, if you head over to 635 and go north, we'll go east when you get to I-30," Jim directed.

As Gene maneuvered the car, merging onto 635, his phone rang. "Barker," he answered, checking his rearview mirror before changing lanes.

"General, this is Mary from Debbie's department."

"Yes, Mary, what can I do for you?" Gene said, accelerating to keep up with the traffic flow.

"We've just learned that you probably had a tail when you left Love Field this morning," she answered. "Did you notice anything unusual?"

"Not really," he told her. "And what do you mean, probably? I thought Debbie had tabs on all of the people involved with this operation."

"I don't know, sir," she replied. "I was just told to call you and relay the information. Debbie had to talk to someone at NSA about something but said I needed to alert you immediately."

"Get her on the phone," Gene ordered. "I don't want any, *probably*. I want definite. Nail it down. Either there is or there isn't a tail."

"Yes, sir," Mary said. "I'll get her right now."

A few seconds later, Debbie came on the phone and said, "General, NSA picked up a rather strange call using our modified voice recognition software, and your name triggered a call to me."

"Why would that mean I'm being tailed?" Gene asked. "By the way, I've put you on speaker so Jim can listen."

"Understand. We think you're being tailed because the man who took the call said, 'I'm on him,'" Debbie told him. "The caller has been identified as one of Lamance's people, but the recipient has never been cataloged."

"Have there been any conversations since the initial contact?" Gene asked.

"We immediately put the new phone into our list of monitored numbers and it has been used several times calling other numbers that aren't in our system," she answered. "The odd thing is that none of these calls have been using either their code or voice altering as has been the normal method of communication with everyone else involved in this operation."

"Do you know the location of any of these new phones?" Jim asked.

"Not yet," she admitted. "It takes a little time to insert the virus, and there have only been a couple of calls where we could gain access to the phone. I expect to have all of them connected to our computers within the hour."

"Any idea of how many people are involved?" Jim asked as Gene took the exit to head east toward Forney.

"So far, just one," Debbie answered. "I've put a priority on getting into his phone and it should be giving me his location any minute now. I'm tracking you guys, so I'll let you know the second I determine his location."

"Was Jim's name brought up in any of the conversations you've intercepted?" Gene asked.

"No, no mention of him," she answered. "This one seems to be centered entirely on you."

"How can you be certain Gene's the target?" Jim asked.

"Because part of the conversation was, and I quote, 'You get that old fat ass General if it's the last thing you do,'" she answered. "Not that I'm just referring to the physical attributes ascribed but running a combination of General and Barker through the system, the only other one that came up was connected with World War II and died several years ago."

"Very well," Gene said before hanging up. "Let us know as soon as you have anything."

"What do you think?" he asked Jim as they saw the sign for Forney. "Should we head back to your house?"

"I say no," Jim answered. "First, if they're following us, that wouldn't do any good. It would only lead them to me as well. And for now, it doesn't appear that I'm a target. I'd say we go on to Christina's and wait there while we eat."

"I'll bring my pistol in, and if Debbie's right about knowing this guy's location any minute now, we'll know when he arrives at the restaurant, and we'll deal with him there," Jim continued. "From what we've been told, this guy may not even know that I exist and won't be expecting me. As far as he's concerned, I'm probably just a dinner guest you picked up, and I doubt if he'll give me more than a cursory glance. That'll give me a chance to decide his fate before he decides yours."

Chapter Thirty-four

"What do you think we should do now?" Gene asked as they saw Christina's restaurant just ahead.

"I'm in favor of going in and then just watching the door to see who follows us," Jim answered. "He hasn't made a play for you yet. I'm not sure what he's waiting for. Maybe he's waiting on someone else. Maybe he's waiting for the optimum shot."

"We've got him," Debbie called. "He's about a mile behind you."

"Any other players?" Jim asked as Gene pulled into the parking lot.

"There hasn't been any chatter on the phones, and we haven't been able to put locators on the ones we're monitoring yet," she answered.

Jim looked at Gene as he parked the car and asked him, "Want to go with my idea?"

"That's as good as any," Gene answered. "Debbie, we're going in the restaurant. Keep us informed."

"Yes, sir," she answered. "He's about a half mile out right now."

"Let's get you inside where you've got some cover," Jim said, changing his plan. "I'll take the phone and wait out here. Right now, he can't see if we both went in, but if we wait any longer, he will. Maybe I can take him before he gets in the building."

"Okay," Gene said, handing Jim the phone. "This sort of leaves me out of the loop, but I don't really see any other option."

"Just get in the restaurant, sir," Jim said, shutting his car door. "I'll move down a couple of cars and pretend I'm talking on the phone when he pulls in. With a little luck, he hasn't had a good enough look at me that I'll get a chance to get close to him before he comes into the building after you."

As Gene disappeared into the restaurant, Debbie called, saying the car was about a quarter of a mile away and slowing.

Jim stood between two cars a little way from Gene's, pulled his pistol from the holster, and jacked a round into the chamber. With the phone in his left hand held up to his ear, he saw a white Honda pulling into the parking lot.

"I've got a car pulling in," Jim said as he looked at the single occupant. "Is that him?"

"The car we're following is pulling in," Debbie confirmed. "If there are no others there, it's him."

Jim stood watching as the car slowly passed where Gene had parked and finally stopped with the driver looking at the restaurant door.

Deciding it was as good an opportunity as he would probably get, Jim came from between the cars and walked across the front of the car trying to appear as if he was going into the restaurant. As he came abeam the driver's window, he glanced at him and nodded his head.

Stopping, Jim held the phone away from his head and mouthed, "Can I help you?" at the driver.

The driver rolled the window down and said, "No thanks. I'm just waiting for a friend."

Jim nodded again, pretending to turn for the building, and pulled his pistol from behind his back. Quickly shoving it through the open window, he fired two quick shots.

As the driver slumped over, Jim jerked the door open and pulled him from the car. Jumping in as soon as he could manage, he slammed on the brakes and put the car in park.

Once stopped, he got out, pulled the driver to the rear door, and put him in the back seat. Getting back in the driver's seat, he drove the car to an open spot near the end of the parking lot.

After parking, he rolled up the window, tossed the keys onto the floorboard, and shut the door. Pausing to put his pistol back in the holster, he pulled his shirttail out and headed to the restaurant.

"Debbie, you might see if there's someone out here that can come get the car with a tow truck," he said, walking in. "I'm not sure who you should contact up there but start with Gene's assistant.

I'll brief Gene on what happened when I get to the table," he told her, spotting Gene at a table near the rear. "But there probably isn't much he can do from here. If he wants to do anything else, he'll give you a call."

Sitting down across from Gene, he handed him the phone and said, "Debbie's calling someone to make arrangements to remove the car. You might want to make a few calls to give your people a heads up."

"What happened?" Gene asked, taking the phone. "I heard a couple of quick pops, but I wasn't sure if it was you or something else."

"That was probably me," Jim answered. "Did anyone else notice it?"

"It's pretty noisy in here," Gene said, looking around. "A couple of people turned their heads and looked toward the door, but that was about it."

"Good," Jim replied. "I did everything I could to keep the noise down, but there's always the chance that someone will hear it. Guess today is my lucky day."

Gene sat silently for a minute before saying, "That's too damn close. It's time to remove the head of the snake."

"I agree," Jim said, picking up a menu. "I'll need to talk to a couple of people to see if we can move my schedule up a week or so."

"You know, this is why I hired you to begin with," Gene said, watching Jim peruse the menu.

"For a lunch companion?" Jim joked.

"No, asshole," Gene told him. "Because you think fast. You make a decision and do it. That's what I saw in the Marine that pulled my nephew from that hill in Vietnam. That's what I just saw today."

As the waitress came toward their table, he finished saying, "I'm sorry I questioned your actions yesterday. Maybe it caused some ripples in my timeline. So did today."

"Well, the best-laid plans," Jim said, handing his menu to the waitress. "I'd like the Carne Asada Shrimp Relleno, medium rare, please. And could I substitute Borracho beans for the rice?"

Chapter Thirty-five

Later, while they were eating, Jim asked, "General, what's the real difference between Black Water and startup companies like Lamance's?"

"I don't have a problem with new companies entering the security business," Gene answered. "We were a startup once ourselves.

Fortunately, we had some very good contacts within the military and other government departments," he continued. "But it was pretty iffy there for several years. Bad publicity damn near destroyed us a few years ago when knowledge of one of our operations was leaked to the public."

"If an operation is abhorrent to the public, why do we do it?" Jim asked. "If an organization can't withstand public scrutiny, why should it exist?"

"You know the answer to that as well as I do," Gene answered. "There are things that must be done to protect the same people that decry what they perceive as cruel or unjust. Let's take Hitler. If someone had eliminated him before he came to power, think of the number of lives you'd have saved.

Closer to home, take David Burke, who took over the cockpit of a Pacific Southwest Airlines flight and ultimately killed 43 people when he crashed the plane," he continued. "What if someone had been on that airplane and killed him before he could destroy so many lives?

Or the guy who walked into a McDonald's in San Ysidro and killed 22 people?" he added. "What if you had seen him getting out of his car with an Uzi, a shotgun, and a pistol? Would you have shot him without a trial?

There are people who would condemn you if you did. And probably want you locked up for taking the law into your own hands," Gene said, shaking his head.

"We can only try to prevent horrendous acts from occurring," Gene continued. "And the best we can do is use the intelligence we manage to get and act as soon as we can."

"Sort of a 'what they don't know won't hurt them' philosophy?" Jim posed. "I know we did things in Vietnam people could never condone. And a lot of things were done during previous wars that resulted in war crimes being charged. I guess my big question is, who determines what's best for the public? Is it some bureaucrat who decides who lives and who dies? Some politicians? The head of some corporation? Who?"

"Ultimately… it's guys like me," Gene answered. "Sometimes the company gets involved in a contract negotiation, and we have to make what's really a moral decision. Sometimes it's guys like you.

Take yesterday," he explained. "You made a decision to end three lives. Who gave you the authority?"

Pausing, he then said, "What about today? What proof do you have that the man you just shot was going to harm anyone? A phone call saying someone was following me?

Maybe it was a process server with a summons from a local judge. How did you know?

The truth is you don't," Gene said. "You assumed, as did I, that the man was out to harm me. You made your decision based on the best information available. If you were correct, you saved my life and potentially the lives of some of the innocent people here in this restaurant. What if you hadn't done it?" he asked. "What if the guy had walked in and started shooting? You can chase that rabbit down the hole for the rest of your life, trying to see if what we do for a living is just. I don't have the answer.

But back to the question of what's different between Lamance's operation and Black Water," Gene said. "We operate with at least the approval of a legally elected government. What Henry's doing is to benefit Henry.

If the company were to ever attempt to get me involved in an operation that I thought was over the line, I'd refuse," Gene told him. "Remember me asking if your pursuit of the men that killed Jennifer was anything other than a personal vendetta? Aren't you making a decision as to who lives or who dies? Are you not doing exactly what Lamance is doing? Operating for your own benefit?

"The bottom line is that all of us have to make a decision as to what's right and what's wrong," Gene said as a man in coveralls with Acme Towing embroidered above a roadrunner walked in, looking around. "That's one of the things I look for in any potential recruit. Whether or not you know it, you do the same. Take North; you rejected him not because you thought he didn't know right from wrong. But because you had reservations about him not acting even when he was right.

Bitterroot, on the other hand, you saw something that led you to believe his definition of right and wrong didn't fit," Gene told him as he waved at the guy looking their way.

"Now that we're done waxing philosophical, I guarantee that sooner or later, you'll make the wrong decision. That's the hell of it. Can you live with your decision after it's done?" Gene asked.

Chapter Thirty-six

Finally heading back to Jim's house in Mesquite, Gene asked, "What's your opinion of why the guy you shot back there wasn't on our radar?"

"I think Henry's running out of people since we started downsizing his organization," Jim answered. "Since he wasn't using any of the safeguards we've seen in all of the previous communications, I have to believe that he's grasping at straws trying to rebuild and hold his organization together."

"I agree," Gene said. "I'm going to look into how he's doing in bidding contracts when I get back to Quantico. I'm guessing he's pretty much stopped if he's short of personnel until he can replace those he's lost over the last couple of weeks."

"I'd also take a look at what's going on with the contracts he had before this started," Jim suggested. "If he's able to fully man those, he can continue operations until he's found replacements. If you discover that he's not fulfilling them, it's a definite sign that he's running out of men and becoming desperate to regain any toehold he had.

Another area to look at is his overseas operations," Jim added. "He may start reassigning people from overseas back here. That would at least get some more experienced people here to counter Black Water."

"I'm not sure he has the ability to do that," Gene argued. "I told you his model was based on using indigenous personnel due to the cost. Most of those people wouldn't be able to operate here. He might be able to pull a few of the supervisory types, but that might not be an option either. Especially if he believes it would damage the little reputation he's gained for his overseas operations. No, I think he's going after former military members who possibly served in one of the Special Forces, like Seals."

"Maybe there's a chance for Black Water to insert someone into his organization since he appears to be hard-pressed to staff his domestic operations," Jim suggested. "Run a check on recently discharged guys that might have the skill set he's looking for and find someone you think he'd hire. If you can get a mole in, you'll have a better idea of what his intentions are."

"I don't think we have time for that," Gene countered. "This latest effort on me tells me that he wants immediate results. So did the renewed attack on you. Desperate men use desperate measures."

"The only other thing I can suggest is what we do, as you mentioned back at the restaurant," Jim suggested as they got to Mesquite.

"What's that?" Gene asked.

"Cut off the head of the snake," Jim told him. "That's been my plan since this started. I was just going to take him last. If he's recruiting as fast as it appears, we'll always be one step behind. And that's not the place to be when your life is in danger. If you want this to come to a successful end as quickly as possible, that's what I suggest."

"You're probably right," Gene agreed as they got to Jim's house. "Every other option will take too long, and sooner or later, he'll manage to take out some of our people. You like to use the risk-reward matrix to make decisions. Well, here's the risk; we will lose someone if we don't shut him down as soon as possible. Reward, we don't lose anyone, and stop the threat against you and me. I don't really see a downside."

"Another reward might be the information we get from him," Jim added. "I'd like to know where my other target is. If that guy knows what's happened to the other men with him in Fort Worth, which I can't imagine he doesn't know, he'll rabbit, and I doubt that even Debbie can find him with all of her voice recognition programs if he's paranoid."

"How soon do you think you'll be ready?" Gene asked as Jim got out of the car.

"I'll know in an hour or so," Jim answered, standing by Gene's open window. "Give me a call when you land back in Virginia, and I should have an answer.

And if you happen to determine where Jennifer's last shooter is, I'll take care of him at the same time," Jim told him.

"I definitely will," Gene said. "And thanks for this afternoon. I didn't really tell you that before, but thanks."

"Don't mention it," Jim said, looking at Gene. "You just keep checking your six. Remember, your opponent doesn't have to be good to win. He only has to be lucky once."

Chapter Thirty-seven

The following morning, Jim called Mike Bitterroot and asked about the preparations they had discussed. Hearing that it would take at least another week, Jim called Gene to give him the update.

"General," Jim said as Gene answered. "I just talked to my guy out here regarding our discussion on timing. I was overly optimistic. It appears it'll be a minimum of a week before I can proceed with my plan for Henry."

"That's the least of our worries right now," Gene told him. "It seems that the entire Lamance operation has gone silent."

"Silent as in shut down or silent as in no communication?" Jim asked.

"Silent, as in no communication at a minimum," Gene answered. "There has been zero communication between known phones and any other phone that we've heard."

"I find that difficult to believe," Jim replied. "Was there anything preceding this silence that would explain it?"

"We're looking into that," Gene told him. "Debbie's group is reviewing every phone call or listening to any conversation that the phones picked up during the last week."

"You want to know what I think?" Jim asked.

"Definitely," Gene said. "Until we figure this out, a lot of our people could be in danger, and we have no way of knowing it or warning them."

"Let's assume that Henry knew about most of the capabilities of Debbie's programs since he worked for the company," Jim began. "That's why he implemented the single-use protocol.

The voice enhancement or modification system he used was to counter her voice recognition program," he continued. "The rudimentary code he was using was just an added precaution in case someone violated the single-use or voice modification directions.

I think he's figured out that his system has either been compromised or there's a new protocol being used that he didn't know about," Jim surmised. "Just think about how quickly we've managed to thwart all of his plans over the last couple of days.

If it was me and I only knew that somehow every time I, or one of my people, were using a phone and it was obviously being monitored, I'd shut down the entire thing," Jim said. "That appears to me to be what's happened. He's probably trying to find some way to communicate that's entirely different than anything he's previously done."

"We've come to the same conclusion," Gene agreed. "The big question is, what's he doing?We all agree that he needs communication and must have found a way to keep us out of the loop.

And, it has to be simple to have been implemented so quickly," he added.

"Has anyone there thought about if he's using a proxy?" Jim asked.

"What do you mean?" Gene asked.

"I'd use someone to talk for me," Jim explained. "Someone whose voice wasn't in the system. Who didn't have the same cadence or vocal patterns I did.

Henry's not stupid," Jim continued. "He's been exposed to or knows about most of our capabilities regarding electronic communications. If I could come up with the proxy system, so could he. It's simple, and it can be implemented immediately."

"I think you're on to something," Gene agreed. "I'll get with Debbie and let her figure out if that's what's going on."

"When you do, tell her to look for phrasing that parallels what Henry used when on the phone," Jim told him. "Even if someone else is speaking the words, they'll probably be exactly what he wrote. I assume he's writing it because he knows we have the capability to monitor any voice within a certain distance of the phone.

I realize that we generally speak differently than we write, but certain words or phrases could be a clue," he continued. "Another thing to look for is a tone after the proxy speaks."

"Why a tone?" Gene asked.

"Maybe the recipient doesn't have a proxy," Jim explained. "To signal that he understands what the caller has said or directed, he simply presses any key on his phone. I don't know if each key has a different tone, but that's something else she can look at."

"I'll get her on it immediately," Gene said. "I'll get back to you as soon as we know something. In the meantime, we can't warn you of any threats, so be extra cautious about your surroundings. Limit your exposure as much as possible.

Vary your daily routines. Go to a different restaurant besides Venice Pizza. And I'd leave that damned 'Vette in the garage. It's too noticeable."

"Guess I'll get a jar of peanut butter, a loaf of bread, some grape jelly, and go hide in the closet," Jim replied. "Of course, I'll need milk, and there's no refrigerator, so I'll need an all-clear before the milk spoils. I just can't drink chunky milk. Not with my PBJ."

"Don't be a wiseass," Gene scolded. "You know what I mean."

"Yes, sir, I do," Jim said, smiling. "And as the saying goes, this ain't my first rodeo. You take care of that; what did Debbie say they called it, *old fat ass*?"

Chapter Thirty-eight

As Jim was rechecking his suitcase for tomorrow's flight, Gene called to tell him they had figured out why there hadn't been any communications involving Henry's company.

"Proxies?" Jim asked.

"You were right," Gene confirmed. "They found that each phone they'd been monitoring received a short call from an unidentified female using an unidentified phone just prior to going silent.

The voice merely said, 'Get a new phone call back',", Gene continued. "Then they traced every call that the 'lady' received and started monitoring those phones. That led to another phone that the 'lady' used to give instructions.

I should have bought stock in Apple or whoever makes cell phones," he added. "This little impromptu buying spree resulted in over two hundred new phones being added to their monitoring list."

"And you're positive this is Henry's organization?" Jim asked.

"Almost one hundred percent," Gene answered. "The number of new phones matches the number of phones they were monitoring but have gone silent. And, they are each within a mile of where the old phone was last used."

"Sounds like you've nailed it," Jim told him. "Guess we're back in business."

"By the way, are they using the tone thing I told you about?" Jim asked.

"Yes, they are," Gene told him. "That was one of the final points that told us these phones weren't being used by normal people talking to each other."

"When does Debbie think she'll have control over these new phones so we can track them and hear conversations when the phone isn't being used?" Jim asked.

"She's installed the listening program in most of them," Gene answered. "But there haven't been any side conversations so far."

"Don't you find that strange?" Jim asked. "If the listening program that can hear any conversation within feet of the phone is in the phone, and there are no conversations being picked up, something's wrong."

"I hadn't thought about that," Gene admitted. "If nothing else, there should be background noises, radio, TV, motor noise, something that would be picked up by the phone. I agree, something's wrong. I'll have her look into that."

"As you know, I'm leaving in the morning for a trip," Jim said. "I've still got the company phone, and I'll keep it on me in the event you hear anything. And I'm going to take a taxi to and from the airport so no one can sabotage my car or put an explosive beneath it.

Since we don't know exactly why these phones aren't picking up background noises, Henry may be running a little diversion with them," Jim continued. "He may have another set of phones specifically for his teams that are hunting our people.”

“That is a possibility,” Gene admitted. “Instead of a taxi, I’ll have a driver and car at your house tomorrow morning to take you to the airport. He’ll also be waiting at the terminal when you get back in three days. What time do you need him tomorrow?”

“I sign in at 7:30,” Jim answered. “Have him here at six o’clock.”

“Done,” Gene said, nodding. “You can coordinate with him regarding your return trip. I’ll work with our other people likewise until we figure out what’s wrong with the phones.”

“Batteries,” Jim blurted out. “I’ll bet they’re pulling the batteries out of the phones when they aren’t being used. That would explain why they go silent when the call ends.

Has Debbie been able to track these phones?” Jim asked. “I’ll bet that it’s intermittent because the phone can’t be seen without the battery.”

“If that’s true, how do they know when they’re being called?” Gene asked.

“Specific times,” Jim said. “Each guy has a certain time frame to have his phone on. Maybe a one or two-minute window each hour or half hour, and he’s told to make sure there’s no noise during that period.

One other thing,” Jim added. “I’m sure the old phones are still being monitored, and I’d be willing to bet that one or two of them are being used for personal calls regardless of being told to destroy them. If Debbie can tie the exact location of the new phone when it’s on to the old phone, she has the user. And that guy may lead her to another, who’ll lead her to another, and so forth. Maybe she can rebuild the organization that way.”

"That's a good idea," Gene admitted. "Maybe you should come to work for her."

"Nope," Jim said. "I'm barely competent to turn on a computer, and even then, I have to look at my notes to perform routine things we have to do to get flight plans or even sign in. And my knowledge of the phone is how to answer it or make a call. And this speed dialing? I'm already punching buttons as fast as I can. Nope, I'll stick with field work."

Chapter Thirty-nine

"How was the trip, sir?" the driver asked as Jim came out of the terminal three days later.

"You know how it is," Jim answered, tossing his suitcase in the rear seat and opening the front passenger door.

Sliding in, he continued. "Come to the airport, put a hundred and something strangers in the airplane, go to another airport, and swap them for a different hundred and something strangers. Then, go to another airport and do it again. And then let the last bunch off at another airport and go to a hotel.

Get up the next morning, go back to the airport, put a hundred and something strangers on an airplane, go to another airport, and swap them for a different hundred and something strangers, and go to another hotel," Jim said, shaking his head. "And then today, we got up at the hotel, went back to the airport, and brought a hundred and something strangers to Texas."

"Sounds something like being a limo driver," the driver said as he pulled away from the curb. "Except we go home instead of a hotel."

"I'd prefer to go home," Jim answered. "But that's not what they pay me for."

"Speaking of going home," the driver said as he headed for the north airport exit, "The General said to ask you if you could go to Love Field, where he has a jet waiting for you instead of going home. He also said it would only be for one day."

Jim pulled out his company phone and called Gene's office. When he answered, Jim asked, "Do you really need me in Virginia? I've been gone for three days; I'm out of clean underwear, and the only civilian clothes I have are a sweaty 'Bull Riders Eat Dirt' T-shirt and a pair of jeans with beer stains."

"The short answer is…yes," Gene answered. "If you insist, I'll have the driver swing by Walmart and you can get clean clothes on the company. One plain white T-shirt, one package of tightie whities, and a pair of jeans."

"Okay, I'll go to Love Field without the lavish offer of the company, but I want your word that I'll be home tomorrow night," Jim told him.

"You have my word," Gene promised him. "There'll be a briefcase on the plane when you get there. The plane's fueled and ready to go. I'll see you when you get here this afternoon."

"Love Field, sir?" the driver asked, smiling.

"Love to," Jim answered, shaking his head.

Arriving at the General Aviation terminal, Jim thanked the driver and grabbed his suitcase. As he entered the terminal, he saw two men with stripes on their shoulders sitting on one of the couches in the lounge area.

Walking up, he asked, "Are you guys waiting for someone to take to Virginia?"

The older man with four stripes rose and extended his hand, saying, "Yes, sir. I assume you're Jim Lashley. I'm Buck Owens, and this fine young man beside me is Tom Crews."

Shaking their hands, Jim said, "You'll have to forgive my attire. I was more or less kidnapped on my way home from DFW."

"I was told you worked for American," Buck said as they headed for the airplane. "We don't have any Flight Attendants, but Tom makes a pretty good Jack and Coke if you're inclined."

"I may have to take you up on that," Jim replied as they boarded the plane. "I'm assuming that I'll have to drink alone, though."

"I'm afraid so," Buck told him, handing him a briefcase. "It's Tom's leg, and he hasn't taken the approved FAA drinking pilot course."

"That's a shame," Jim said, grinning. "It's a requirement with American to have the Drinking Pilot Rating along with an Airline Transport Rating. If you want an airline job, you better learn to drink."

"So I hear," Tom said, walking to the back of the airplane and showing Jim where the drinks were stored. "Please help yourself."

"I only have one request," Buck said before going to the cockpit.

"What's that?" Jim asked, putting his suitcase on the floor beside the seat.

"Don't let me see the bottle," he answered.

"Why? Is there a company rule against alcohol on a company plane?" Jim asked.

"Oh, good lord, no. That's part of the minimum equipment list," Buck told him as he smiled and stepped into the cockpit. "It's just that the sight of Jack Daniel's makes my mouth water, and I can't stand watered-down whiskey. Let me know if you need anything."

"You do know that FAA stands for 'Formerly Alcoholics Anonymous,' don't you," Tom said, following Buck into the cockpit.

Chapter Forty

After landing at Quantico, Jim was met at the airplane and taken to the Black Water headquarters. As he passed through the enhanced security measures, a member of the Black Water staff wearing the typical black knit shirt with their logo above the left breast pocket escorted him through the maze of halls to Gene's office.

Entering, he heard the General telling someone to send the information to him as soon as possible. Hanging up, Gene said, "Sorry to interrupt you on your days off, but I thought you needed to see exactly what's happening regarding the Lamance operation."

"Come with me," he said, stepping from behind his desk. "This'll be easier to explain from Debbie's area.

Following him down another maze of halls, Jim asked, "I'm guessing that this isn't something you couldn't tell me after I got home."

"I could have, that's true," Gene said, pushing open a door into a large room full of huge screens covering one wall. "But I think you'll understand why I wanted you here after you see what's developed over the last two days."

"Jim, good to see you," Debbie said, coming up to him with her hand out to shake. "I want to personally thank you for the little idea of the Lamance operation using proxies. Even if we'd thought of it later, we've been able to locate just about every operative we knew about before much sooner."

"Good to see you too," Jim said, shaking her hand. "I'm glad it helped."

"And the other thing about comparing phone locations, that's been a real benefit," she continued, leading them to the front of the room to look at the screens. "I was surprised at how many of their people did, in fact, violate a directive about destroying the old phone…anyway it made my job much easier."

"What we're looking at here," she said, sweeping her hand across the screens, "Is the location of every known Lamance operative. They're depicted as red figures. There are several white figures we believe to be either the increased use of proxies for communication or new agents we haven't confirmed. I'm leaning toward proxies since they seem to always be paired with the same red figure."

"The green figures are our people," she said before turning back to face them.

"Impressive," Jim said after a glance. "But why did I need to fly up here to look at where people are that could, and probably will, change before I get back to Mesquite?"

"Did you notice the small numbers within the different figures?" Gene asked. "If you didn't, take another look. While you're doing that, you'll probably notice a larger black figure with the number one."

"Okay, I see that," Jim said, looking from screen to screen. "I also see that different areas of the world are on the screens."

"So you can see that the black number one figure is in the European country of Bulgaria," Gene told him.

"I see that," Jim replied.

"These screens are currently dedicated to the Lamance operation," Gene informed him. "And the number one figure represents Henry Lamance."

"He's left the country?" Jim asked, staring at the screen. "Why?"

"We believe the answer to be twofold," Debbie answered. "First, if you'd seen the locations of his people three days ago, it was a dramatically different scenario. Several of his people have been shifted from overseas back here. I believe that he's over there trying to hold his operation together while he recruits new people to replace those he brought back to the States."

"The second reason I think he's left the country is that he believes, correctly, that he's being targeted here at home," Gene added. "We intercepted several messages to him advising him of an attempt on his life within the next week."

"Any specifics?" Jim asked.

"Just you," Gene answered.

"Why would he single me out?" Jim wondered, looking at the number of red figures within a 50-mile radius of Dallas.

"Personally, I think it's because you've been involved with more than any other of our people in, as you put it, downsizing his operations," Gene told him. "And I'm not discounting the possibility that we have a leak."

"Are you talking about the one you already know about?" Jim asked, turning from the screens.

"At least him," Gene confirmed. "We've also intercepted a conversation regarding one of the people in Debbie's section that revealed someone in his family was being watched and he needed to provide certain information or, how did he put it?"

"He'll need a revolving account at the local florist," Debbie added.

"I can see how Henry found out who was statistically more likely to be after him simply because of the numbers," Jim said, shaking his head. "Maybe he's connecting the dots between the men I've removed that were involved with Jennifer's death. But to leave the country and abandon his tentative chance at operations here? I think that's a bit of a stretch."

"What if I told you the conversations we've intercepted contained the word 'Bitterroot'?" Gene asked. "Would that narrow the stretch for you?"

Chapter Forty-one

"Let's go grab something to eat," Gene suggested as Jim contemplated the bombshell that Mike may be targeted.

"If they know about Mike, then they probably know about North," Jim posed as they headed to the cafeteria.

"Quite possible," Gene agreed. "But his name wasn't in any of the conversations."

"How do you see the operation against Henry now?" Jim asked, entering the cafeteria.

"I'm shifting the responsibility to Dark Water operations," Gene answered. "As long as he's over there, he's their problem."

"Does that mean I need to postpone my plan for him?" Jim asked as they took trays from the start of the food line.

"Yes, definitely," Gene replied as they selected their meals. "Especially since Mike may be compromised. Possibly targeted."

"I'll give him a call when I get home and tell him to drop everything," Jim decided as they took their trays to a table as far from the others as possible. "I certainly don't want to be responsible for risking him or a member of his family."

"We can always revise our plan if Henry comes back," Gene told him, setting his tray on the table. "I know you wanted him for yourself, but as long as he's overseas, my hands are tied."

"What if you transferred me to Dark Water for a specific operation?" Jim asked. "That would keep the operation under their control."

"I don't think that's feasible," Gene told him. "First, by the time we got you over there, he may be back here. Second, you've still got another of his people here that you want. And finally, if we send you to Bulgaria, it could take days to get close enough to remove Henry. So, my answer is for you to stay here and let me worry about him. At least for now."

"Okay," Jim begrudgingly agreed. "What's the status of my other project?"

"He's currently down in San Antonio," Gene answered. "There's been some communication leading us to believe that he's there for an operation targeting one of our assets in that area."

"How good is your intelligence regarding him?" Jim asked. "Do you believe he'll be there long enough for me to get down there and remove him?"

"We think so," Gene answered. "He's one of the people who kept his old phone, and we're getting more details about his plans. But we haven't heard anything definite regarding a timeline."

"Does our man know about the threat?" Jim asked as he finished his meal.

"Of course," Gene said, placing his fork on his empty plate. "And we've made arrangements to move him and his family to another location until we think the threat's been removed."

"And that brings me back to you," Gene added as they took their trays to the cart holding used plates and utensils. "I promised I'd have you home tomorrow. I'll do so. But, I'd like to send you to San Antonio to work with a team we're putting together to resolve the threat to our man we've been discussing."

"When do you want me to leave?" Jim asked as they headed back to Gene's office.

"I've briefed the folks down in San Antonio that I'd try to have you there by noon tomorrow," he answered. "But it's your decision. I know you'd like to have a day or two at home, but I think this is a chance for you to close the chapter on Jennifer's killing."

"Who's in charge down there?" Jim asked, taking a seat across from Gene's desk.

"Randy Scott," Gene answered. "He's been with us several years in more or less an intelligence position. But, as luck would have it, he knows the lady who's been the proxy for one of Henry's people who's been operating in San Antonio for almost a year."

"But he doesn't have any operational experience, does he?" Jim asked.

"No, that's true," Gene answered. "And I told the team down there that you'd run the operation once you arrived. That is if you want to go."

"When do I leave?" Jim asked, eager to get a chance at the last of the shooters who killed his wife.

Chapter Forty-two

After landing at Love Field, the plane waited for Jim to take a taxi to his house and get clean clothes before taking him to San Antonio.

The minute Jim walked into his house, he knew someone had been there. There was nothing truly out of place, but little things like a drawer not quite closed or clothes in the closet pushed closer together than usual as if someone had been looking behind them.

As he walked out of the house, he pulled his phone from his pocket and made a quick call to Gene. As it was answered, he explained what he thought had happened and said, "I can't go to San Antonio today. It'll take me a couple of days to go through the house and see what was done."

"You don't think it was a break-in and robbery?" Gene asked.

"Not a chance," Jim answered. "There was a couple of hundred dollars in a drawer in my bedroom that's still there. I'm going to get one of the local security companies here to come do an electronic sweep of the house."

"Don't do that," Gene ordered. "I've got a contract down there with someone who can be there within the hour.

Let me call him and then call you back. What are your immediate plans?"

"Just wait for your guy, I guess," Jim answered. "Maybe go grab a bite to eat."

"Don't use your cars," Gene advised. "I'll let Craig, he's the owner of the security company I'm calling, know that there's a possibility of explosives either in the house or one of the cars. Just sit tight for a couple of minutes until I can get Craig's people over there."

As Gene hung up, Jim pulled out his private phone and started to dial the number for Mike. As soon as he turned it on, he heard a definite sound that he'd never heard before. It sounded like background noise, except it was absolutely quiet where he was standing. Hanging up, he switched back to the company phone and called Gene.

"Connect me with Debbie," he said. "I think my phone is bugged."

"Your company phone is," Gene answered. "You've known that since we worked the El Paso problem. How else were we supposed to track you and set up a communications network with the other team members?"

"I'm talking about my personal phone," Jim explained. "I want to know if the company is monitoring it as well."

"Hang on, I'll get her in here," he said.

Minutes later, he heard Debbie's voice saying, "Jim, this is Debbie. I'm here in Gene's office, and we've got you on speaker. Tell me why you think your private phone is bugged."

"I turned it on and started to dial, but there was a hissing noise, maybe sort of like static," he explained. "I just hung up without dialing and called Gene. My question is whether or not the company is involved?"

"I can assure you we aren't," Debbie answered. "But what you're describing is more or less classic for rudimentary phone tapping."

"How can I be sure if it's safe to use it?" Jim asked.

"I just got off the phone with Craig," Gene told him. "I'll call him back and tell him to make sure he brings whatever he needs to check your phone."

"That's fine," Jim said, shaking his head. "But I'd like to know how long this has been going on and whether or not I need to get a new phone."

"I really doubt if we can determine how long it's been being tapped or bugged," Debbie told him. "But we can electronically wash the phone if you want to keep it. However, my best advice is to get a new one and a new number. I realize the issues involved with contacting everyone, but you saw how easy it was for me to screw with every new phone the Lamance group used.

I doubt anyone else outside of the company or NSA has this capability, but changing your number will put them back at square one," she continued.

"Who have you called in the last few days that we need to contact?" Gene asked. "We need to make sure they're aware that their phones may be bugged."

"Hang on while I look through the recent call list," Jim said, turning on the phone.

"Turn it off!" Debbie yelled immediately. "If there happens to be a listening program inserted that's activated when the phone is on, they can hear everything you say."

As he was turning it off, Jim walked to the side of the garage and dropped the phone into an empty trash can. Walking back to the front of the house, he told Debbie and Gene what he'd done and asked, "If it has the same program you have, he could have been listening to me even if it was off, correct?"

"That's correct," Debbie answered. "But that program is much more sophisticated than a simple wiretap, which is what I suspect. However, that's the safest thing for now."

"Let's get back to who you've called that we may need to contact," Gene directed. "Other than friends or the airline, have there been any calls to someone involved with our organization?"

Thinking back over the last week or so, he suddenly said, "Mike Bitterroot and Butch North. I've used that phone to call both of them."

"That may explain the intercept we got mentioning Bitterroot," Gene surmised. "But, if they got his name, why not North?"

"I'd bet they got it also," Debbie said. "Unless they were tapping Bitterroot's phone, and that led them to Jim's phone."

"We're betting on peoples' lives," Jim told them. "How do we get the word to them that their phones may be bugged and they're likely being watched?"

"You know where they live; you need to get a car and get out there," Gene told him. "The San Antonio project is on hold until we figure out how many people Lamance has caught in this web. I'm calling a rental agency we have a contract with to bring you a car and to tell the pilots waiting for you to come back here. You wait there for Craig and get him working on your house, cars, and that phone.

Then, when the car's delivered, head out to North's and make sure he's aware of the issues," Gene continued. "Then Bitterroot."

Debbie jumped in, suggesting he stop off for a throwaway phone to use until he could replace the old one.

"Since you don't plan on using it again, I think it's safe to turn it on and write down the numbers you want to keep. But realize it may be monitoring everything it hears."

"Got it," Jim said, heading back into the house. "After I get a gun, I'll take care of that. And I'll give the phone to Craig to see if he can figure out what was done."

"I'll have him send it to us," Gene said. "You get going, but take a good look at anything you need to open or lift while you're getting your pistol. It wouldn't surprise me if they've booby-trapped your house while you were on the trip.

And, since they're probably wondering why something hasn't happened since you were supposed to be home yesterday, be extra vigilant about any cars in the neighborhood or following you when your car is delivered," Gene advised. "Looks like Henry's tossing everything he can at you. And, by extension, anyone you may have contacted since he's set his sights on you."

"Got it," Jim said as he looked for trip wires or anti-lift devices when he opened the closet and started to take the box holding his gun from the back of his closet.

Taking a sheet of paper from his nightstand, he tried to slip it beneath the box. When it stopped sliding, he quit pushing it and returned outside.

"We have another problem," he said, walking from the house. "I think there's an issue with where I keep my gun."

"Why's that?" Gene asked.

"There's something between the box and the floor," Jim said as he saw a van with Craig's Security Services pull up to the curb. "And I'd noticed that the clothes on hangers in that closet were bunched up when I was checking the house before.

Craig just got here, and I'm going to tell him I think there's a bomb in the house. He may want me to call the police bomb squad," Jim continued. "I'll call back when things are a little more under control."

Chapter Forty-three

"You must be Jim Lashley," a man in multi-pocketed cargo pants said, walking up. "I'm Craig. General Barker said you had a problem."

"Nice to meet you," Jim said, shaking his hand. "I'm not sure exactly what the General told you, but I'm sure someone's been in my house while I was gone. I also believe there's possibly an explosive of some sort beneath my gun case in one of my closets."

"Why would you think that?" Craig asked.

"Let's just call it a hunch," Jim answered. "I wanted to let you know there's a possibility before you went in. If you'd prefer for me to call the police's bomb squad, that's fine with me."

"Have you attempted to move the gun case?" Craig asked.

"No. I tried to slide a sheet of paper beneath it to see if there might be an anti-lift device," Jim explained. "The sheet got about a third of the way, and something obstructed it."

"We'll take a look at it," Craig said, nodding. "If it's something we can't handle, I'll call the bomb squad. I've worked with them several times and know all of them very well. Anything else?"

"I need the house and garage also checked for any explosives, even if the one in the closet turns out not to be one. And check for any electronic stuff," Jim answered.

"Everything unlocked in the house?" Craig asked as he told a technician to get a sniffer for the possible explosives.

"Probably not the back door," Jim answered. "I can open the garage if you'd like."

"We'll take care of that," Craig told him. "If there are explosives, we'll look for them before we start opening doors or looking under cars. Sometimes, there's a dummy for you to find to take your attention away from the real threat. For now, I'll assume any closed door is potentially a threat."

"How much time do you need?" Jim asked as a black Suburban pulled to the curb with a small four-door sedan following.

"Don't have a clue," he answered. "Depends on what we find inside. But, a minimum of five hours to sweep for electronics and explosives. Add time to remove any electronics or dismantle any explosives we find; it could run into twice that much."

"Right now, I don't have any way for you to contact me," Jim said, watching as a man got out of the suburban. "I've got to leave, but if you need anything, contact General Barker, and he'll call me."

"No problem. If you get me the phone, I'm supposed to send it to Quantico, I'll get busy," Craig said as the technician came from the van. "I'll let the General know when we're done and what we find if you're not back."

"Thanks," Jim said, turning to a man walking up the driveway carrying a clipboard.

"Are you Mr. Lashley?" he asked as Craig headed for the house.

"Yes," Jim said.

"The keys to the Suburban are in the ignition; if you'll just sign here, please," he said.

After handing Jim a copy, he said, "Just call the number at the top when you're ready, and we'll come get the car. Have a nice day."

As the man walked back to the waiting car, Jim went to get the phone he had put in the trash can and walked back to the house. Taking a pen from an end table in the living room, he turned on the phone and wrote Mike and Butch's numbers on a pad of paper. Tearing off the sheet, he turned the phone off and walked through the house looking for Craig.

Finding him in the bedroom where he'd been told to look for the explosive, Jim handed him the phone and asked, "Find anything in the closet?"

"Semtex," Craig said as the technician left the room. "Looks like they put a sheet of it under the gun case. We'll see what we need to do once we figure out how it's armed. As soon as my guy can get suited up, we'll take care of it."

"Good luck," Jim said, turning to leave. "It would be nice to have a house to come home to. And I'm sure your guy would like to make it home in one piece himself."

"It'll be all right," Craig told him as they left the room. "He's ex-Navy EOD, explosive ordnance disposal. Sometimes, I think he relishes finding something to play with. Gotta be nuts to want to mess with crap that'll blow your lips off if you breathe wrong."

Chapter Forty-four

Jim left Craig to take care of his house as he headed toward 635 and hoped both Bitterroot and North were all right. Pulling into a Best Buy on Mesquite Drive just off 635, he went in and bought three prepaid cell phones.

Back at his car, he loaded Mike and Butch's numbers in the one he would keep for himself and put his number in the other phones. Driving away, he tried Butch's number but got his message box. Trying Mike's, he got the same result.

Now more worried than ever, he used the company phone and called Gene.

"General," he said as Gene answered. "I've tried to call Mike and Butch. Neither one answered. I'm not too surprised that Butch didn't. He could be on a trip. Anyway, I've got a new phone, and I'll send you the number when I get to Butch's house. I also got phones for him and Mike in case their phones are tapped."

"That sounds good," Gene told him. "Quick update on San Antonio. We've moved our operative and his family to ensure their safety until we can get back on track."

Pausing, he continued, "I'll use a contact with American to see if I can determine if North is on a flight and call you when I find out. Maybe that'll save you a trip to his place."

"All right, I'm probably an hour from there," Jim said, merging onto 635 headed north. "I'll plan on stopping there first if I don't hear from you."

"Be careful out there," Gene reminded him. "Both places are rather remote, and any response for help would most likely be too late to help if you get in trouble."

"That's for sure," Jim said, approaching the exit for I-30. "The worst thing is that I'm unarmed and will be until I can get to Mike's and borrow one."

"Hang on a second," Gene said. "I'll make a quick call and see if I can't get you something right now."

A couple of minutes later, Gene was back on the phone saying, "There's a Cash America Pawn shop just off 635 on Centerville Road. You can probably see the sign from the road before you get to it. A man by the name of Renaldo runs it. He'll have a package for you when you get there. Let me know when you're back on the road."

"I see it now," Jim said as he moved to the right-hand lane to take the Centerville exit. "I'll call when I leave there."

Pulling into the pawn shop, Jim went and walked to the counter where a single man stood working with a pistol.

"Renaldo?" Jim asked as he approached.

"Yes, sir," Renaldo said. "How may I help you?"

"A friend of mine just called," Jim answered. "Gene Barker. Said you could help me with a pistol."

"Ah, the General," Renaldo said, smiling. "I'm working on his request right now. You must be Jim."

"Yes, sir," Jim replied. "Do you need some identification?"

"That won't be necessary," Renaldo said, laying the pistol on a rubber mat. "The General said you would be here within five minutes when I spoke with him. And you're the only one matching his description that's here. But if you feel the need…"

"If you're happy, I'm happy," Jim answered. "What did the General ask for?"

"He asked for me to provide you with a close-range self-defense weapon," he answered. "The rest he left to my discretion."

"And what have you decided I need?" Jim asked, looking at the pistol.

Picking it up, Renaldo said, "This is the Sig Sauer P320 9mm. In my humble opinion, the best home defense weapon available, except for a Browning 12-gauge pump with double ought buckshot. This particular weapon also has a crimson trace sighted for 50 feet. If you shoot at 25 feet, you'll be about a quarter of an inch high. Seventy-five feet, a quarter of an inch low.

I've tossed in two full clips and a box of Winchester Defender Elite 147 grain JHP ammo," he continued. "This should be sufficient to ensure the protection of you and your loved ones."

Handing the pistol to Jim, he asked, "Will there be anything else?"

"I don't think so right now," Jim said, feeling the weight of the pistol. "Is it all right to put a clip in here in the store?"

"No problem," Renaldo answered. "Although I'd prefer for you not to load one in the chamber until you are outside."

Pointing the pistol at the distant wall, Jim put pressure on the handgrip and saw a red dot appear about chest high. Bringing the pistol back down, he slipped in a clip, he felt the balance, and asked, "How much do I owe you?"

"Nada," Renaldo said, smiling. "The General has taken care of it."

"In that case, thank you," Jim said, gathering up the extra clip and box of ammo. "Perhaps I'll return next time I'm in need of your expert opinion for another weapon."

"I still recommend the Browning 12 gauge," Renaldo reminded him as he turned. "Maybe saw a little off the barrel and shorten the stock. Very nice for vermin."

"I'll keep that in mind," Jim said, opening the door. "If I ever have a vermin problem."

Chapter Forty-five

Jim rejoined 635, looping around the top of Dallas until joining 114 north of DFW. Heading west, he was approaching the town of Trophy Club when Gene called. "Yes, sir," Jim answered as he maneuvered to the left lanes.

"North is on a trip," Gene told him. "Not due back until tomorrow. Let me know what's happening at Bitterroot's."

"I'll be there in about an hour and a half," Jim answered. "I'll call as soon as I know. And thanks for the varmint killer."

Thirty minutes later, he joined 287 going north toward Decatur. Now an hour away and light traffic, he pushed his speed up to ten miles an hour over the posted limit.

At Bowie, he headed southwest on 59, hoping he remembered how to get to Mike's place with all the small dirt roads. Seeing Farm Road 1288, he remembered heading north on it for a couple of miles and then making a left turn by a big green 'Bulls 4 Sale' sign.

Seeing the sign, he turned on the gravel road and spotted Mike's place about half a mile ahead. As he turned in the gate, he started looking for anything out of place. Seeing nothing except Mike's old red pickup, he stopped in front of the house and made sure his pistol had a round in the chamber.

Easing the car door open, he looked to see if anyone was looking out of the windows of the house. Seeing nothing, he quietly shut the car door and walked toward the red pickup.

Approaching it, he checked out the area behind the house. Still seeing nothing, he eased to the side of the house and peeked into the window into the kitchen. Not seeing anything, he headed down to the barn, where he thought he heard a motor running.

As he got to the back, he saw Mike with a helmet on welding two pieces of pipe together. Knowing that the sound of the welder running would drown out anything he said, he walked around to the front of where Mike was welding and waited for him to lift his head.

A few seconds later, Mike looked up and pulled the welding rod from the spot where he'd been working. Lifting his helmet, he said, "Hey, Jim. What's brought you out here?"

"Checking on you," Jim answered. "Can you shut your welder off for a few minutes?"

As the motor stopped, Mike asked, "Is there something wrong?"

Trying to find a way to broach the subject, Jim finally asked, "Do you know anyone working at Quantico?"

"My sister's husband works somewhere up there. Why?" he asked.

"Your name came up in a conversation that was being monitored," Jim told him.

"My name," Mike said, frowning. "Why would my name come up in a conversation up there."

"You remember the conversation we had when I came out with Butch," Jim started. "Well, there's an organization that's helping me look for the guys who killed my wife."

"What organization?" Mike asked, taking off his helmet and gloves.

"That doesn't matter," Jim answered. "But as they were listening to some of the people they believe were involved, one of them told someone, I'm assuming your brother-in-law, that a member of his family was being watched. Have you seen anything out of the usual in the last couple of days? Any unexpected visitors? Strange cars?"

Mike thought for a second and said, "One of the guys at the auto parts store in Bowie said someone had been in asking if he knew where I lived a few days ago. Other than that, nothing."

"But nobody's been out here that you don't know," Jim asked, looking into Mike's eyes. "Even just driving by."

"Not that I've seen," Mike answered. "But I can't see the road from back here. And I damn sure can't see or hear anything when I'm working. What the hell would anyone want with me?"

"I'm afraid that's my fault," Jim confessed. "The people I've been hunting are now hunting me. And anyone I've been in contact with over the last couple of weeks.

I just learned that my phone's been bugged, and they probably know everyone I've called," Jim continued. "Since I've called both you and Butch, they may be connecting you to what I've been doing."

"If they bugged your phone, they might have bugged mine as well," Mike said. "And Butch's."

"That's why I brought you a throwaway," Jim said. "It's prepaid and already has my number in it. If I need to call you, I'll use it. Use it to call me if you need to. Is your phone at the house?"

"Yeah, let's go get it," Mike said, heading toward the house.

Jim followed him to the back door and said, "I'll go get the other phone from my car and meet you inside."

Handing it to him when he came into the living room, Jim asked, "Can I see the other phone?"

When Mike gave it to him, he turned it on and heard the same background noise he'd noticed on his. Holding it up for Mike to listen, he asked, "Do you hear that noise? That's the same noise mine was making."

"I hear it," Mike said, nodding. "It's been making that noise for a couple of days. I thought it was something to do with the crappy reception we get out here. Are you sure that my phone's bugged?"

"Not positive," Jim answered, shaking his head. "But that's the sound mine made. I've got a security guy checking my house, and he's sending my phone to be checked. You might want to get someone out here to check yours."

"I'll do it," Mike said, looking at the phone. "Who the hell cares who I talk to or what I say?"

"Probably the same guy who was asking where you live," Jim answered. "My advice is to just watch what you say using that phone or get a new one. And really pay attention for the next few days. I may be getting paranoid, but too much strange shit has been happening, and I'm worried that I may have drug you and Butch into it."

"I'll keep an eye out," Mike said, tossing the phone on the couch. "Are you going by Butch's house?"

"He's on a trip," Jim answered. "I'll get with him when he gets back. Anyway, I'm sorry I got you involved in my problems, but I've got to get back home to see what the security folks found."

"Don't worry about getting me involved," Mike said, sticking out his hand. "I've been looking for some excitement anyway. Semper Fi."

Shaking his hand, Jim nodded, saying, "Semper Fi, my friend," as he headed for his car.

Chapter Forty-six

Pulling out of Mike's driveway, Jim called Gene to give him an update. "Mike's fine," he told him. "I think his phone was tapped, and I gave him one of the prepaid phones to call me if he needed to. Then he told me someone was asking about where he lived.

But he says he hasn't seen anyone around his place or seen any strangers," Jim finished. "I'm not sure if the caller saying Mike was being watched knew about what we'd discussed or if it was just a probe."

"We looked into it this afternoon, and we're pretty sure it was just that, a probe," Gene told him. "The call came out of nowhere, and Jonathon, Mike's brother-in-law, says he had no clue why he was called. I'm guessing Henry's people are looking for some way to recruit another inside guy to either replace the one we've known about or to verify his information."

"How'd they zero in on him?" Jim asked.

"Probably because their intelligence picked up the Bitterroot name and ran it against anyone with connections to Black Water," Gene surmised. "Their intelligence isn't near as good as ours, but public records are easily accessed, as you well know.”

“Oh, yeah,” Jim agreed. “That’s why Jennifer disliked Debbie when they met. Debbie knew our entire history together merely from searching public records.

By chance, did you ask Jonathon if he’d be willing to work with us regarding misdirecting Henry?” Jim asked, heading south on 287.

“Yeah, however he wants a little time to think about it,” Gene answered. “He’s concerned that he might be putting his wife and Mike in jeopardy if they catch him lying.”

“I can understand that,” Jim said, nodding. “And I don’t blame him if he doesn’t want to get involved.

“How do you plan on giving North the phone you bought for him?” Gene then asked.

“I thought I’d swing by his place when I get down to Rhome,” Jim answered. “His ranch is only a couple of miles out of my way, and I’ll leave it just inside the gate. Have you contacted him since we found out about the phones being tapped?”

“No, but I’ll get a message to him at his layover hotel this afternoon to have his phone checked and that you’ve left one for him,” Gene answered.

“Not to change the subject, but is Henry still out of town?” Jim asked as he passed through Sunset.

“Yes, and before you ask, your other friend is still down south,” Gene answered. “I think you might want to concentrate on that.”

Pausing, he continued, “I’m waiting to see if he relocates since his purpose for being down there has moved. Now, if you’ve got nothing else, I’ve got other fish to fry.”

"No, that's about it," Jim answered. "Just wanted to update you on Mike and see what had been found at my house."

"Craig can tell you when you get home," Gene said before hanging up. "But keep in mind that they may not be done with you. Now's not the time to relax."

As he came to Rhome, Jim joined 114, heading west toward Aurora, where Butch lived. Making the left turn on 718, he quickly came to the closed gate leading to his house.

Pulling in, he parked and grabbed the prepaid phone from the seat. Getting out of the car, he walked to the gate and put it behind the post where the gate latched.

As he turned to go back to his car, he caught a glimpse of something shiny where the gate was hinged. Walking across the driveway, he bent down to see if he could figure out what it was.

There were two wires loosely connected just below the bottom hinge. Following the wires down below the fence, he saw a small wooden box that was almost invisible in the tall grass. Unsure of what he was seeing, he decided to call Gene back and let him know about it.

"Yes, Jim," Gene said, answering. "What is it? I thought you were heading home after dropping off the phone."

"That was the plan," Jim told him. "But I've found something suspicious here at Butch's place. Maybe I'm being paranoid again, but there's a box below his gate with a couple of wires leading to the hinge where they connect."

"Give me his address," Gene quickly responded. "I'll see if Craig can get out there to take a look or knows someone discrete out there to take a look. Can you hang out somewhere close by until I call you back? Somewhere a couple hundred yards from the gate?"

"There's a feed store just across the road where I can wait and see anyone coming to the gate," Jim said, walking back to his car. "This shit's getting irksome. Maybe it's time to get Dark Water busy before anyone else gets hurt."

Chapter Forty-seven

"Craig has a guy coming out of Fort Worth," Gene said when he called back. "Should be there in half an hour."

"I'll be watching for him," Jim replied. "I'm wondering if Henry's people know when we're flying. He obviously got into my house when I was. Now, Butch comes back from a trip to find his gate rigged. And maybe his house."

"That's as good of a scenario as I can come up with," Gene agreed. "Maybe he has people in American's network, same as we do."

"Or he could be putting people on the ground to see when we leave in our uniforms," Jim suggested.

"A waste of man hours," Gene argued. "Maybe with Mike since he's more or less retired and the window of opportunity to do something is much smaller. I'll stick with someone at the airlines."

"What really bothers me is that neither of these guys would be involved if it hadn't been for me," Jim lamented. "Maybe I shouldn't have been so hell-bent on taking care of those shooters myself. None of this would be happening."

"Hindsight," Gene told him. "But you can't be sure it's because of that. We've got people under watch or targeted that had nothing to do with your downsizing operation.

It really doesn't matter," Gene continued. "It's the old 'why did the chicken cross the road' question. Who gives a shit. The damn chicken is over there. Doesn't matter why. Just deal with the situation you have now."

"That's true, but I can't help but feel responsible," Jim argued. "The desire to inflict as much pain and to let Henry know ahead of time exactly what horrors he was going to experience is why Mike and Butch are involved. If I'd just stepped up to him and put a bullet through his head as I did the others, these guys wouldn't have gotten involved."

"And if you'd never married Jennifer, she wouldn't have been involved," Gene scolded. "You have to take the good with the bad. As much as I miss her, I've got memories that can't be taken away that I wouldn't have had."

"I signed on for this life," Jim said. "She didn't. Neither did Mike or Butch."

"Don't give me that crap about her not signing on," Gene told him. "She signed on to your life knowing Marines die. That's what we do. Maybe she didn't know about what you're doing now, but she would have stuck with you if she had. Life has no guarantees, you know that. Sometimes it sucks, sometimes it's a peach. We do the best we can to protect our loved ones, but sometimes it's out of our hands.

Now all we can do before more of our friends or family are placed in danger is to try to wrap up this operation," Gene finished. "I know you wanted Henry, but I'm sending instructions to catch him and either cancel his ticket over there or bring him to me. "I'm not going to risk another one of my people by letting him exist one day longer than I have to."

"Hey, I see a van pulling up to Butch's gate," Jim said. "I'll call back when I get a chance."

Hanging up, he started the car and crossed the road to park behind the van as the driver was getting out.

"Excuse me," Jim said, jumping out of the car. "Who are you?"

"I'm Chad," he answered. "I was sent out here to look at a suspicious package. Are you the guy who called Craig?"

"Sort of," Jim told him. "I'm the guy that discovered it."

Walking across the front of the van, Jim pointed to where the box was sitting in the grass. "I called a friend who knows Craig and asked for someone to come look at it."

"Guess I'm the lucky guy," Chad said, gently moving the grass around the box. "But if you don't want to be the unlucky guy, you might want to move back across the road. I'll let you know when it's safe to come back."

Nodding, Jim backed up his car and returned to where he had been waiting. As he sat watching, his prepaid phone rang. Knowing only two people would be calling that number, he surmised it would be Mike since the other phone was across the road.

"Mike," he answered. "What can I do for you?"

"Just thought I'd let you know; I caught some asshole messing around in my house," he answered. "Not sure what he was doing, but the story he's telling me is that he got lost and came in to see if he could use the phone."

"Hang on to him," Jim said. "I'll make a quick call and see if we can't help you determine who he is and why he was in your house."

"He's not going anywhere," Mike replied. "I convinced him to have a seat at the kitchen table, and he was very obliging when I taped his arms behind him and his ankles to the chair legs.”

“Comfortable, sweet cheeks?” Jim heard Mike asking as he took the company phone from the seat.

“I’ll call you right back,” Jim said and hung up.

“General, I’m going to need a favor,” he said as Gene answered.

“What do you need now?” he asked.

“Mike just caught someone in his house,” Jim said. “I’m going to guess it’s one of the same group that was in my house and that left the package here at Butch’s. Is there any way you can get someone out to Mike’s to get the man before Mike’s short fuse burns out?”

“Give me a minute,” Gene answered before hanging up. “I’ll make a call and get back to you.”

Seeing Chad waving, Jim left the car parked and headed across the road. “What did you find?” he asked as he got to where Chad was holding the wooden box in his hands.

“It was an IED,” Chad said, opening the top of the box. “An improvised explosive device. And a very amateur IED at that.”

“The box was lined with Semtex, which could have been all right,” Chad explained. “But he put it on all four sides instead of just the back where it would direct the blast toward the driveway.

He used a couple of pounds of ball bearings for shrapnel, which could certainly do some damage,” he continued. “But with the blast going every direction, he wouldn’t get the effect he wanted.

The other thing that tells me this guy was an amateur was the triggering device,” Chad explained. “He was depending on the movement of the gate to pull the wires apart. However, when the gate opened, it would actually shorten the distance from the wire to the detonator instead of getting longer. In other words, the wiring was on the wrong side of the gate post and wouldn't have separated as required to set off the Semtex."

Jim stood looking at the box and finally asked, "Would you mind going up to the house and checking it for any explosives or electronic devices?"

"Do you have a key?" Chad asked, carrying the box to the rear of the van.

"No, but I'll get you into the house," Jim answered. "Except we'll have to walk since I don't know the gate code."

"That's no problem," Chad told him, putting some equipment in a tool belt. "I've got everything I'll need to sweep the house. If I find anything, I'll come back to get it. Given the quality of work this guy does, I doubt there's much in the house."

"Thanks," Jim said, walking to the fence. "I hope you're right, but since you're here, I'd rather not take a chance on my friend walking into a trap."

Chapter Forty-eight

As Jim and Chad were walking up the driveway to the house, Gene called. "Yes, sir," Jim answered. "What did you decide to do about the guy at Mike's?"

"Call him and tell him that a helicopter from Carswell will be landing at his place in about 30 minutes," Gene told him. "There'll be a couple of my men on board who'll take charge of the guy he caught. Make sure Mike understands that we want this man unharmed. He's the first one we've caught that's been involved in the planting of these explosives."

"Are you talking about mine and here?" Jim asked as they arrived at the house.

"More," Gene clarified. "My office has received calls from all over the country that IEDs are being found at several locations involving our people. I think Henry is going for one massive operation to remove as many of them as he can as quickly as he can.

We've been out gunning him one-on-one, so he's upping the stakes," Gene continued. "Now it appears that he's trying to conduct a massive strike using explosives with no regard to who's injured. I want that man at Mike's to get any information I can to see just how extensive this operation is."

"I'll give him a call right now," Jim said as he broke the glass in the rear door window. "I'll get back to you as soon as I talk to him."

"What was that sound I just heard?" Gene asked. "What's happening out there?"

"I broke the window in Butch's back door," Jim explained. "I wanted to get his place looked at in case they planted something in here. I'll explain it to Butch when I talk to him."

"Fine," Gene said. "Just make sure Mike doesn't do anything until the chopper gets there."

As the line went dead, Jim opened the door and told Chad to go see if anything had been placed inside.

Calling Mike, he walked to the garage and looked at the side door while waiting. Seeing nothing unusual, he opened the door and saw Butch's 'Vette sitting there.

"Mike," he said as he answered. "There's a chopper on its way to get the guy you're holding. It's very important that we take this guy into custody. He may be our only means of getting information about several explosives being planted around the country."

"What do you want to know?" Mike asked. "I'll make sure he talks and get anything you want me to ask."

"Don't do that, Mike," Jim told him. "I don't know exactly what questions to ask, and you don't either. Please, just turn him over to the guys coming to get him. They should be there in 20 minutes or so. Just make sure he's able to talk when they get him."

"Okay," Mike reluctantly agreed. "But I want to know why he was here."

"I'm going to guess that he's there to plant some sort of explosive like they did at my house. And Butch's. But I'll make sure we find out," Jim assured him. "And I'll make sure you know what we find. Just wait for the chopper and help them if they need it."

"If that's what you want," Mike told him. "I'll let them have this piece of shit when they get here. But, if he causes any problems, there are no guarantees."

"Thanks. Just try to make sure nothing happens to him until then," Jim said before hanging up.

As he was heading for the house, his prepaid rang. "Hello," he answered and waited to see who had called.

"Jim, this is Debbie," she said. "I just wanted to let you know we're now tracking you and Mike. Also, we've activated the listening program so we can monitor any conversations the phones pick up. So, if you run into trouble, just let us know. You won't have to do anything that might raise suspicions if someone is with you."

"Thanks," Jim told her. "Have you done the same with Butch's phone I left?"

"No, it has to be activated before I can program it," she told him. "If you want to get it and make a call, I'll take care of it before he gets back."

"I'll get it when we go back down to the gate where I left it and call my phone. How much time do you need?"

"A couple of minutes will do since we know the number," she answered. "We'll be waiting."

As Jim was hanging up, Chad came out and said, "There doesn't appear to be anything. I did a pretty quick run-through, but nothing jumped out. I'm 99 percent certain that the house is clean."

"That's good enough for now," Jim replied. "Let's get out of here. When will we get something regarding what you found at the gate?"

"I'll send my report to Craig, and you can get it from him," Chad said as they headed back up the driveway to his van. "Is there anything else before I go?"

"That'll do it," Jim said. "Thanks for coming out."

Chapter Forty-nine

With nothing else he could do at Butch's, Jim headed home. Approaching Roanoke, Gene called, telling him they had picked up the man Mike had been holding.

"How was he?" Jim asked.

"Pretty good, considering," Gene said, almost laughing. "Mike decided to assist our guys when they got there. There are a couple of hairless areas on his arms and legs where the tape was ripped away. And it looks like one of his shoulders was dislocated, lifting him from the chair."

"That sounds pretty minor compared to what I think Mike would have enjoyed doing," Jim agreed. "Where are you taking him now?"

"I've got a team flying down to Carswell who'll conduct the initial interview," Gene answered. "Once they determine there's nothing more to learn, we'll bring him up here until we determine his ultimate fate."

"Anything new on the other folks who've had IEDs found in their homes or other areas?" Jim asked as the traffic became heavier approaching Trophy Club.

"There's been one casualty and one minor injury," Gene answered. "One of our guys hurried home after we notified everyone what was going on, and he surprised one of their guys while he was planting a bomb in the man's garage.

When he hit the remote garage opener, the bomb exploded, killing the guy who was planting it," Gene continued. "A piece of metal flew out and hit our guy's arm through his open car window. It took three stitches to close the wound."

"How many of these incidents have we had?" Jim asked.

"We've discovered almost 50," Gene answered. "But I expect at least twice that many before it's over."

"Who are they targeting? Is there any pattern so we can narrow our focus?" Jim asked, passing through Southlake.

"The best we can determine is most, but not all, of the targets have been with the company since Henry worked here," Gene told him. "I'm guessing he compiled a list of operatives before he left. Possibly names of people to approach for employment with his company. I don't think he was planning to eliminate our people back when he first started his company, but we may never know."

"You said most," Jim questioned. "Who are the others? What's their connection to us?"

"You answered that question earlier," Gene reminded him. "People like Mike and Butch. People whose names popped up while surveilling the people he knew worked for us."

"What's your guess as to how long it will take the team from Quantico to *debrief* the man Mike caught?" Jim asked.

"Not too long," Gene answered. "They should be there in three or four hours and take over. The Base Commander at Carswell was kind enough to provide a facility to detain our guy that's rather isolated from most of the base.

The guys we're sending down have years of experience at debriefing," Gene continued. "They start out pretty benign, and things are pretty rosy if they get any cooperation. But they'll ratchet up the discomfort level fairly rapidly if they don't.

We don't have the luxury of time," he added. "I want all the information this man has before we lose anyone. We've been extremely fortunate up to now, but the infamous golden BB will find a target sooner or later.

So, I've made my wishes known, and they'll compress the process down to a matter of hours instead of days," he said. "And you'd be surprised at how quickly someone becomes extremely cooperative when you strap them down and wrap a towel around their face and keep a steady stream of water being poured over their nose and mouth.

A side benefit is there's no visible damage," Gene explained. "And, once they've experienced it, they offer little resistance if they're strapped down again with a couple of guys standing by with a towel and pitcher of water."

"I'm going to bet it won't take long with this guy," Jim responded. "Hell, he may not need much encouragement. Chad, the man Craig sent to Butch's house, said the IED at the gate was very amateurish. If Henry's having personnel recruiting problems, the replacements he's getting aren't of the same caliber as the ones we're removing."

"That seems to be the case," Gene agreed. "The reports I've been getting from across the country are pretty much the same. Oh, there's the occasional professional job, but mostly definite signs of unskilled people. Hell, I'm pretty damned surprised that more of them haven't blown themselves up."

"You buy cheap crap, you have cheap crap," Jim responded. "But that's fortunate for us."

"Not necessarily," Gene argued. "Amateurs tend to make mistakes that involve people outside the operation. A true professional will be surgical. The amateur uses an ax when a scalpel is required. Collateral damage is never good for a business like ours. It draws too much attention, and our customers pay us not to be in the news. Bad for them, bad for us."

"Unlike El Paso, where we mounted a body count surpassing a Rambo movie?" Jim argued.

"Question: how many non-players were involved? Answer, none," Gene told him. "Who took the blame? The same gangs that have been a cancer on El Paso for decades.

A high body count doesn't necessarily mean it wasn't a surgical strike," he argued. "Look at the body count we're amassing today. A pittance compared to El Paso, but the only newsworthy ones aren't attributed to us. Fortunately, even the ones due to Henry's inept operatives have been blamed for other reasons, such as turf wars. A company like ours only exists because we're in the shadows. Even we couldn't survive in the light of day. That's one reason Henry's doomed to failure. We just have to get him out of the picture before he brings us down as well."

Chapter Fifty

Craig was putting everything back in his van when Jim pulled up to the curb. "Everything good?" he asked, following Craig back into the house.

"Clean as a newborn baby's butt," he answered.

"I'm not sure I'd consider that really clean," Jim replied. "Although I've never had kids, some of the stories I've heard…"

"Then I'll just say there are no listening devices or other electronic measures in the house, garage, or any of the cars," he clarified. "Nor are there any more explosives. By the way, if you ever decide to get rid of that little 'Vette, I'd be willing to discuss it."

"I'll let you know," Jim said, smiling. "But you may be too old for a driver's license before I let her go. Been in the family far too long."

"Thought I'd ask," Craig said, shrugging his shoulders. "I sent your phone to Quantico; it should be there in a couple of days. I'm also going to send them a detailed report on the explosive we dismantled as soon as I get a chance to see if I can locate the vendor of the switches and the Semtex. They can take it from there if they want to pursue it."

"Oh shit!" Jim exclaimed, taking out his new phone. "I've got to notify the airlines that I've changed my contact number. Is there anything else?"

"Not that I know of," Craig answered. "I'll send you a complete report when I get back to the office. I've briefed the General, and I'll send the bill along with his copy of the report. Just let me know if you ever need us again."

As Craig was finishing up and his technician joined him, Jim called Crew Scheduling at American. "Good afternoon, Patricia," he said as she answered. "This is First Officer Lashley, and I need to give you guys a new contact number. My other phone is on the fritz, and I'll use this one until it's fixed, or I get a new one."

"Good," she told him. "I see here that we tried calling you about an hour ago. Guess that's why we didn't get you. Go ahead with the new number, and I'll update your contact information."

After giving her the new number, he asked, "Why were you trying to call me?"

"Flight Standards needs your flight tomorrow for a new First Officer's IOE," she answered. "That is if you absolutely don't want to stay home and get paid."

"No, I always put the needs of the company ahead of my own," Jim told her, laughing. "Have you ever had someone who didn't want to give up a trip?"

"Actually, yes," Patricia said, laughing as well. "There was a Captain who absolutely did not want to be removed from a trip. Found out later, through the grapevine, he was having a little romance with one of the Flight Attendants on that trip."

"She must have been absolutely stunning," Jim told her.

"I'm not sure exactly how stunning *he* was," she explained. "The Captain was removed from the trip, but he non-reved the entire sequence."

"Ah, true love," Jim replied. "Ain't it grand?"

"It's something," she answered. "Anyway, I've taken you off the trip and updated your phone. Your next trip is still scheduled for a week from tomorrow. Is there anything else I can help you with?"

"No, ma'am," Jim answered. "Thank you."

"My pleasure," she replied before hanging up.

As the van was leaving, Jim called the number for the car rental agency and told them to come get the car.

Then, using the company phone, he called Gene and told him about being removed from the upcoming trip.

"A little birdie told me that was going to happen," Gene said. "That's why I've been putting together a team down in San Antonio."

"A little birdie," Jim said, shaking his head. "The company must have flocks of little birdies since you seem to know what's going on with American's flight schedules more than I do."

"There you go with your conspiracy theories again," Gene replied. "Now, since your house is safe to occupy and you have nothing to do for almost a week, would you be interested in driving down to San Antonio tomorrow?"

"Since I don't have anything else going on, why not," Jim answered. "How much information am I going to get when I get there? Or is this another by-the-seat-of-my-pants operation?"

"This one is extremely well planned," Gene answered. "I've spent hours with the other team members reviewing the most minute details of where you'll meet them."

"That's it?" Jim asked. "All I get is a location to meet the other members of the team? Where are the details?"

"I could send you a copy of the menu for the restaurant," Gene answered. "But since you've been to a Denny's so often, you probably know it by heart. And they're all the same.

No, really," Gene said, laughing. "Randy will have a package for you as well as the standard equipment. They've been watching the subjects for a couple of days along with Debbie's folks, and they do have a tentative plan.

The only reason I'm getting you involved is because of your interest in one of the subjects," Gene continued. "The guys down there are perfectly capable of executing this operation without you, but I know how you feel about this particular individual."

"I appreciate it," Jim said. "What time do I meet the team, and where?"

"The Denny's in Schertz is just off I-35. Take the exit for 3009, Natural Bridge Caverns Road and it's about two blocks down on the access road after you cross 3009. You'll see the sign," Gene answered. "The other guys will be there at noon. It's about a four-hour drive, so you can get a good night's sleep before you have to leave."

"How long do you think I'll be down there?" Jim asked.

"I'm hoping only one day. Two at the most," he answered. "But you know how these things go. Flexibility is the key to air power."

"And indecision is the key to flexibility," Jim countered, nodding. "And lack of information is the key to indecision."

"There you go," Gene told him, laughing. "The less you know, the more flexible you can be. That's why we

don't give you any more information than you absolutely
need. Call tomorrow if you run into any problems."

Chapter Fifty-one

Jim was just south of Waxahachie the next morning when Gene called. "Do you have time for an update on the guy we picked up at Mike's?" he asked. "Of course you do. You're barely out of Dallas with at least three hours of sitting in your car staring at the open road."

"Other than when I get to Austin, you're pretty accurate about this drive," Jim told him. "What did you discover that you didn't already know?"

"I'll start by saying that the man, Floyd was his name, didn't provide much resistance at all," Gene answered. "Our guys spent less than thirty minutes asking questions that he continued to evade or tell complete lies that were immediately disproven.

When they pulled the curtain away from where they had put the tilting table, his eyes opened wide, and they thought he was having a heart attack," Gene said, laughing. "When they strapped him to the table, he kept screaming, 'I'll tell you anything you want to know. Just ask me. Anything."

"How long did they pour the water on his face?" Jim asked, imagining the scene.

"They never did," Gene answered. "Not a single drop. "He started answering the questions they had asked. Then he started telling them things they hadn't asked. Our guys had a hard time keeping up with everything he was saying. Good thing they had it on tape."

"What was his background, and how did he get involved with Lamance?" Jim asked.

"He spent four years in the Coast Guard," Gene answered. "A friend of his from the Coast Guard had been recruited in some admin function and got him an interview."

"What did he do in the Guard?" Jim asked. "They don't really have what I'd call an offensive force."

"He started out as a Gunner's Mate," Gene explained. "But after finishing the schools, he was more of an electrician than anything."

"Did he know anything about explosives or small arms?" Jim asked as he changed lanes to let traffic merge from the southbound US 77 join I-35 heading south.

"Not after the basics he was taught in school," Gene told him. "We asked him what training he had received from Lamance, and the answer was none. All they were provided with were manuals or pamphlets with instructions on the assembly or positioning of explosives. And absolutely no firearms training or range work."

"Unbelievable," Jim responded, shaking his head. "Sounds like Henry is really having trouble recruiting. I wonder how many more guys like Floyd he's using?"

"Floyd didn't know anything about many of the others," Gene told him. "Other than a couple he met during the initial interview. They were mainly guys who had served one hitch in either the Army or Air Force."

"Did he know of any other targets?" Jim asked.

"Nope," Gene answered. "At least Henry is keeping a tight lid on that. Guess he's afraid we'll find out and make it more difficult for him to continue his plans."

"What are you going to do with Floyd now that he's of no further use to you?" Jim asked.

"He'll have to disappear," Gene answered. "I said from the beginning that anyone actively involved with either the execution of an attempt on our people or the planning of it would pay the ultimate price.

I sure can't just let him go. He might even resurface and come back after us," he continued. "And we're not operating an incarceration facility. I don't have many options in this case. We're just not set up to take care of prisoners."

"You could always send him back to Mike," Jim suggested.

"No, I don't think we need his assistance on this," Gene told him emphatically. "Besides, if Floyd just disappears, it raises too many questions from family or friends. I think the best thing would be a single-car accident. There are some dangerous roads out there in Montague County."

"And a lot of deer crossing them at night," Jim added. "Surprising how many cars run off the road trying to avoid them."

"And lots of narrow bridges," Gene said. "I'm surprised that there aren't more accidents out there. Anyway, I'll check back with you when you get to Schertz and talk to the other guys. Drive carefully and watch out for deer crossing the road."

Chapter Fifty-two

After hanging up with Gene, Jim called Mike. "Good morning," Jim said as Mike answered. "Anything exciting out there in the boondocks?"

"Just another glorious morning in paradise," Mike told him. "All that's missing is the smell of cordite and the distant sound of cannon fire."

"Oh, you do paint a picture," Jim said, laughing. "Anyway, I've got some news for you."

"Good news?" Mike asked. "I don't want any bad news to spoil the start of my day."

"I'll just give you the news, and you can decide its impact on your day," Jim answered.

Pausing, he then said, "The guy you caught worked for the organization we're dealing with and was out there to plant an explosive. A young man by the name of Floyd. And I think you'll find this interesting; young Floyd was a brother-in-arms."

"He was a Marine?" Mike asked incredulously. "That's bullshit. No way."

"I didn't say he was a Marine," Jim corrected him. "I merely said brother-in-arms."

"What the hell does that mean then?" Mike asked.

"The Marines are part of the Navy, aren't they?" Jim asked.

"Unfortunately," Mike begrudgingly answered. "So, he was a Navy puke."

"Not quite," Jim corrected him. "He was one of the elite members of a small military branch closely aligned with the Navy since they can be part of it during wartime."

"All right, I give up," Mike told him. "Just tell me who the hell he was."

"Coast Guard," Jim answered, unable to keep the humor from showing.

"You've got to be shitting me," Mike exclaimed. "No wonder. You know the guy actually peed his pants? I didn't know it until we hauled his pussy ass out, but he pissed himself here in the chair where I tied him. No wonder. Coast Guard. I should have known."

"I thought you'd get a kick out of that," Jim told him. "Apparently, he quickly decided to confess his sins when he saw what the guys from Quantico had prepared for him."

"What happens to him now?" Mike asked.

"I'm sorry to have to be the one who breaks the news, but he'll unfortunately hit a deer on a back road out there," Jim answered. "Tragic, but life can sometimes be cheap."

"Why don't you bring him back to me?" Mike asked. "I've finished that trap you wanted and have a couple of really nice boars that would love to become acquainted with him."

"I'm afraid we can't do that," Jim told him. "Religious issues."

"What religious issues?" Mike asked.

"You're aware that certain religions prohibit eating pork," Jim explained. "Floyd could possibly fall into that category. So, to make sure we don't violate any of his religious principles…well, you know."

"I wasn't going to make him eat pork," Mike explained. "I was going to let the pork eat him."

"Sorry, Mike," Jim told him. "I guess this hasn't been such good news after all. But look at it this way. You bested one of the elite members of that branch of our armed services that included such illustrious members such as Alex Hale."

"Alex who?" Mike asked.

"Alex Hale, Junior," Jim answered. "He was the skipper of the S.S. Minnow. Surely you know your nautical history."

Pausing, he then said, "You probably know him better as 'The Skipper'."

Waiting a couple of seconds and not getting a response, he finally added, "The S.S. Minnow? The 'Skipper'? Come on Mike, *Gilligan's Island*?"

"Oh, screw you, Lashley," Mike said. "You think you're so damn funny. Now my day is ruined. I should have known you'd have some wiseass answer."

"Just trying to inject a little humor in your morning," Jim said, smiling. "But I do want to thank you for catching the little prick and letting us have him."

"Yeah, sure," Mike told him. "Keep me from having any fun with the little Beta Boy before I give him to you. Then you try to make it all right by jerking me around with some old TV crap. I'm not sure I want to talk to you anymore today."

"Maybe Santa will bring you something special this year," Jim responded. "You've been such a good boy."

"It better be something very, very special," Mike told him. "After all the sacrifices I've been forced to make. I'm not sure his sleigh is big enough to make up for the disappointment I feel right now."

"I'll put in a good word," Jim told him. "But right now, I've got to get back to work. I don't have the luxury of being a gentleman of leisure such as you. Take care, my friend."

Chapter Fifty-three

Just under three hours later, after crawling through the unbelievable traffic in Austin, Jim pulled into the parking lot at Denny's.

Walking in, he looked around and spotted three men drinking coffee at a table in the rear. As he neared them, they nodded and pushed the remaining chair out.

"Jim Lashley, I assume," one of them said. "I'm Randy Scott. Have a seat.

How was the drive?" he asked as Jim sat down.

"Not too bad," Jim answered looking at the other two men sitting with him. "A bit crowded around Austin, but not unexpected."

"I live up there, and a bit crowded is putting it mildly. It sucks day in and day out," the man to Jim's left said. "I'm Roberto Mendez."

Shaking his hand, Jim said, "I'm sorry about that. I live just outside Dallas, and I thought I had it bad."

"I'm Marty Robbins," the man across the table said. "I'm from Laredo, and our biggest traffic issue is on Friday night when all of the college kids try to cross the border. I try to avoid that bridge anyway, but weekends…no way."

"I live out in Bandera," Randy told him. "Nice, quiet little place, but I seem to spend a lot of time in San Antonio. I guess there are traffic problems just about anywhere people congregate."

"Have you guys eaten?" Jim asked, picking up a menu and looking at each of them.

"We've been waiting for you," Randy answered, waving for a waitress.

"Sorry to keep you waiting," Jim said, looking at the breakfast choices.

"Gentlemen, are you ready to order?" the waitress asked, taking her ticket book from her apron.

"I'll have the Southwestern Benny Breakfast," Randy answered, handing the waitress his menu.

"Santa Fe bowl, please," Roberto told her. "And some salsa on the side."

"Classic Benny Breakfast," Marty said. "Pico de Gallo on the side."

"I'll take the Country Fried Steak and Eggs," Jim told her when she looked at him. "Eggs over medium and Tabasco, please."

"I'll have it out in just a few minutes," the waitress said, scribbling the last of the orders on her ticket. "And a fresh pot of coffee."

As she walked away, Jim asked, "What's the status of my man?"

Watching the waitress leave, Randy answered, "He's got an apartment in New Braunfels. He's been talking with two guys who are staying in Universal City. They're the ones who've been watching for their target to come back."

"When will that happen?" Jim asked.

"He's back," Randy answered. "We're planning for the two guys here to see him at the Golden Corral, where they normally have lunch. Debbie's people are monitoring their phones and will let us know when they decide to go there.

Once they're in the restaurant, the man they're after will come in," he continued. "We expect they'll notify your guy in New Braunfels as soon as they spot him. He should come down I-35 past us, heading for Universal City. He'll most likely take the exit a couple of miles south of the one you took. That's where we'll wait. There's an exit just down from here before that one, and Roberto will wait here with Marty in case he takes it.

Once he gets on Universal City Blvd, we'll follow him to the restaurant," Randy finished. "We'll take him out there before he goes in if everything works out. If not, we'll just have to make adjustments."

"What about the two guys inside?" Jim asked. "What's your plan for them?"

"We'll either take them when they come out to see what happened, or Marty and Roberto will follow them," he answered.

"How's the timing going to work?" Jim asked as he saw the waitress coming with a pot of coffee.

"Shouldn't be any problems," Randy answered as the waitress left the pot on their table. "We've made trial runs from the apartment in New Braunfels to the restaurant using every possible exit and street.

The range is from twelve minutes to twenty," he explained. "The most likely is the one I just described, and it's fifteen with normal noon traffic."

"So, the two guys here go to the Golden Corral, get the buffet, and take a table," Jim surmised. "Our guy walks in, and they spot him. Let's assume they would normally take about thirty minutes to eat, and so would our guy.

They make their call about five minutes in, and my guy heads down here," he continued. "Give him five minutes to get to his car and fifteen minutes for him to get to the restaurant. That's twenty-five minutes from when the first two guys walked in. I don't think you've allowed enough time since we're going to be a few minutes behind.

You're also assuming they'll wait for the guy coming from New Braunfels to kill our man," he added. "What if they don't wait? I'd be more comfortable if we had someone at the restaurant waiting for the first two guys."

Randy looked at Marty and Roberto and finally said, "I guess you two better get your meals to go. If we're all sitting here eating when we get the call from Debbie, Jim's right. We can't get to the Golden Corral in time if the two guys there want to shoot our guy."

Signaling for the waitress, he told them, "Sorry, guys. Better safe than sorry. Just leave the stuff in the car and go enjoy the buffet."

Chapter Fifty-four

"Do you know our guy that's going there?" Randy asked after their meals had arrived.

"Not really," Jim answered, shaking Tabasco over the cream gravy covering his chicken fried steak.

"Name's Ed Harvey," Randy told him. "I've never met him, but I read his biography the company sent. One tour in Vietnam flying OV-10s. Went to work for Southwest Airlines. Joined the company about ten years ago."

"I'm familiar with the OV-10 Bronco," Jim replied. "We had them in 'Nam. Forward Air Controllers thought very highly of their capabilities. I even worked with a couple while flying the F-4s."

"But I'm more interested in the guy I'm after," Jim said, looking at Randy. "What can you tell me about him?"

"His bio is rather sketchy," Randy answered. "Harold Jackson. Army. Worked in various construction jobs after his enlistment was up. Spent some time as a small arms trainer at a gun range in Houston. It seems he went to work for Lamance about three years ago. He's mainly just a shooter. Not much on the planning phase.

The company said we're to let you have him," Randy continued. "Any particular reason?"

"He's one of the four men involved with shooting and killing my wife," Jim answered. "Matter of fact, he's the last of them. Other than Henry, who ordered the hit on me, all four of them will have gone to their afterlife if I get my chance today."

"What's your plan after we meet them at the restaurant?" Randy asked as he scooped some salsa onto his hash browns.

"I'd like to be in the parking lot when he arrives," Jim answered. "If I can catch him in his car, he'll never leave it. My main goal is to take care of it outside of the restaurant. If I can't, we have the potential of eight shooters in there, and we could lose control of the situation."

"I only count seven," Randy countered. "Three bad guys and the four of us."

"If you were Harvey, would you be there without some protection?" Jim asked. "I damn sure wouldn't."

"No, I wouldn't go in unarmed," Randy agreed, handing Jim an earpiece. "Speaking of that, we need to get a quick com check with Quantico."

When his call was answered, he said, "Good morning, this is Randy in San Antonio for a final com check."

"Good morning, this is Mary," the voice said. "If everyone's on, we'll do a roll call."

"The only one I don't know about is Harvey," Randy told her. All of my guys and Jim are ready."

Mary paused while she was connecting all of the phones to her system and started, "Harvey, acknowledge."

"Harvey," he responded.

"Mendez," she said.

"Mendez," came the response.

"Robbins," she called.

"Robbins," he answered.

"Lashley," she then called.

"Lashley,' he answered.

"Did everyone hear the other people?" she asked. "If you didn't hear anyone's response, let me know."

After hearing that everyone had, she said, "Starting now, we'll be on hot mic, so watch your language. I have all of your locations displayed, and all of the targets are still stationary at their residences. I'll give you a shout when any of them move."

"Good morning, gentlemen," Gene said, coming online. "How's the operation coming? I see from your locations you've made some changes."

"Yes, sir," Randy told him. "Jim didn't want Harvey walking into the restaurant solo."

"I didn't either," Harvey announced. "But I'm just the decoy. Sometimes I feel like that damned mechanical rabbit at the dog races. A pack of hounds chasing me, wanting to rip me apart, and I'm depending on someone to keep me one step in front of them. Not well within my comfort zone."

"It's resolved now," Jim told him. "Here's what I aim to do if the targets do as Randy expected. I'll take Jackson when he arrives at the restaurant in the parking lot if possible.

Mendez and Robbins will be in the restaurant watching the two guys there," he continued. "I'd rather not have you be involved unless one of our guys is in trouble, Harvey. But, if you determine it's necessary, take care of the problem."

"I didn't get a chance to talk about the two in the restaurant with Jim," Randy jumped in. "Does the company still want them taken in or removed?"

"Remove them," Gene directed. "But take them out of the area if possible. Let's try to keep this as low profile as we can. If any of you see a situation developing that's too far astray from the current plan, give us a call and we'll reevaluate. Now, do any of you have any other questions for me? If not, good luck and stay safe. Remember, we're trying to destroy them to keep them from destroying us. Keep that in mind before you take any unnecessary chances."

Chapter Fifty-five

Finishing their meals, Randy and Jim were discussing their former military careers when Mary announced, "We have movement. The guys in Universal City are heading for their car."

"Harvey, where are you?" Jim asked, signaling for the check.

"I'm in a church parking lot about a half mile from the restaurant. On 218, Pat Booker Road, just south of Kitty Hawk Road," he answered.

"Mendez, are you guys in the restaurant?" Jim asked.

"Affirmative," he answered. "We're at a table in the back where we can watch the door."

"Mary, will the targets pass Harvey on their way to the restaurant?" Jim asked as the check arrived.

"That's the closest route," she answered. "They're leaving the parking lot now. I'll know more when they make their first turn."

"Harvey, if they come by you, give them five minutes and then head to the restaurant," Jim told him, putting enough money on the table to cover the tab and tip.

"When you get there, wait for Mendez to let you know when they're at their table," he continued, motioning at Randy for them to leave.

"Where are you going?" Mary asked.

"We're going down the service road so we can watch if Jackson takes the first exit coming south to go to the restaurant," Jim answered as they headed for the door.

"There's a Starbucks about half a mile down on your right," Mary informed him. "That'll put you about 500 feet from where he'll exit. If he doesn't take that exit, the next one is about another half mile further south. I'll let you know when he's approaching the first one."

"Okay, we're on our way," Jim said, sliding into the passenger seat of the Suburban.

"The two are heading southwest on 78," Mary advised them. "That should put them on Pat Booker in four or five minutes. That's just a mile or so south of Harvey."

"There's a clean gun in the glove compartment for you," Randy told Jim as they pulled out of the parking lot onto the service road. "It's loaded with Federal 147 grain HST, and you'll have nine in the clip when you load one in the chamber."

"Is the restaurant crowded?" Jim asked, taking the 9mm pistol out of the glove box. "Are there any empty tables by yours?"

"Maybe half full," Robbins answered. "There are two booths next to us, one on each side."

"Good, let's hope they chose one of them," Jim said as they saw the Starbucks just ahead. "If it works, I want you guys to slide into the booth with them and let them see your weapons after they call Jackson. Then you'll lead them out. Again, low profile and hopefully no shots fired in the restaurant."

"Targets turning on Pat Booker; you should see them in less than a minute, Harvey," Mary said.

"Looking," Harvey answered.

Seconds later, he announced, "I've got a green Toyota with two coming my way. That's the only car in sight."

"They're a half mile from you," Mary told him.

"That's got to be them," Harvey said. "I'll wait here for Mendez to tell me they're in the restaurant."

"They'll be there in a couple of minutes," Mary told them. "I'll let you know when they reach the door."

"Mendez, are you and Robbins ready?" Jim asked as they parked in the Starbucks lot. "The show is about to start."

"We're ready," Robbins answered. "A family of four just came and took one of the booths by us."

"We'll have to be careful with people that close," Jim reminded them. "We're okay if the two take the other booth. At least there'll be your booth between you when you join the targets at theirs."

"They're in the parking lot," Mary announced.

"Keep in mind that these guys are probably armed," Jim reminded them. "I know you think Jackson is going to be the shooter, but they may decide to act before he gets there. Don't hesitate to take them out if they pull any weapon after Harvey comes in."

"They're at the door," Mary said.

"We see them," Mendez answered. "They're just looking around. Looks like they've spotted the booth beside us. Yeah, they're coming our way."

"Harvey, are you on your way?" Jim asked, chambering a round in his pistol.

"Leaving now," he answered. "I'll wait in the lot there until they get their meals and sit down."

"They just took the booth," Mendez said. "And the waitress is coming over to them."

"Not to question your professionalism, but does everyone have a round chambered?" Jim asked. "I'd hate to lose a second when you really need to take a shot."

"We're good," Robbins said as Mendez nodded affirmatively.

"I'm good," Harvey answered.

"They're heading to the buffet line," Mendez announced. "They're right behind the family that took the other booth. Looks like they may be delayed while the kids make up their minds."

"Want me to go on in?" Harvey asked.

"No, I don't want to take a chance of them recognizing you while they're behind that family," Jim told him. "Let's just stick with the plan. No need to rush anything right now. And please make sure you don't make eye contact with either of them when you get in. I don't want them to get suspicious if they think you've noticed them. And take a seat as far from them as you can."

"They're at the line," Mendez told them. "Looks like the kids finally got their pancakes, and they're headed to their booth."

A couple of minutes later, he said, "Our guys are coming back to the booth. Damn, you should see all the food they've piled on their plates. There's enough food there for a platoon of Marines. Okay, they're taking their seats. I'd say any time now for Harvey."

"I'm going in," Harvey said, getting out of his car. "Watch my back, guys. If I'm going to be shot in a restaurant, I'd prefer it to be at least a Ruth's Chris Steak House, not some cheap ass family buffet. And preferably after I've finished a rare filet mignon with a glass of

Chiappini Guado de Gemoli Super Tuscan. If I gotta go, I want to go in style and elegance."

"And I suppose you want an elegant, tall blonde dinner partner, too," Jim said, smiling at the gallows humor as he sat waiting for the countdown signaling his part was about to begin.

Chapter Fifty-six

Mendez was looking at the booth where the two men were eating when Harvey walked in the door and turned away to find a table. After taking a seat with his back to them, Harvey spoke to the waitress and rose to go to the buffet line.

Almost immediately, one of the men said something to the other one while looking at Harvey. As the second man looked, Mendez said, "He's reaching down. Not sure what he's reaching for."

"Hold on," Jim said. "Make sure it's a gun and not his phone before you show your weapon."

A second later, Mendez said, "Phone. We're good."

"He's calling Jackson's number," Mary said almost at the same time. Pausing for a few seconds, she told them, "He just told Jackson that their target was there."

"What did Jackson say?" Jim asked.

"He told them to watch him and wait until he got there," she answered.

"Good," Jim said. "That's what we want. Mendez, you and Robbins have about fifteen minutes to get them out of there. Make damn sure they don't get a chance to use their phones."

"Can I be of any help?" Harvey asked.

"Head for the door," Jim answered. "Maybe that'll draw them out, and we won't have to pull any weapons in front of the civilians in the restaurant."

"Mendez, you and Robbins be ready to follow them if both get up to leave," Jim continued. "Decide who'll stay if only one of them follows Harvey."

"I'll go out," Mendez said. "Are you ready, Harvey?"

"Let's go," he answered as he left the line and headed toward the exit. "I'll have my gun out as soon as I'm outside. Just let me know if you see him pulling his."

"They're both getting up," Mendez said as they watched. "We'll be right on their ass when they hit the door."

"Jackson just got to his car," Mary told them.

"Give me a call when he's five minutes from me," Jim told her. "What's your status, Mendez?"

"We'll be at the door in a minute or so," he answered. "Harvey, where are you standing?"

"I'll be to the right of the door when you walk out," he told him. "I'll take the first one who comes out." "No shots if you can help it," Jim said. "Mendez, get on top of them as they open the door. Give the trailing guy a good hard shove as soon as they step out. With a little luck, he'll go down and take the first guy down with him.

Robbins, be ready to get their phones as soon as you can," Jim said. "Harvey, you and Mendez get their guns."

"Jackson is heading for I-35," Mary said. "I'm guessing he's ten minutes from you, Jim."

As the first of the men stepped out of the door, Harvey said, "Hey, asshole. Looking for me?"

Just as he turned to look at him, Mendez shoved his partner behind him as hard as he could. As the man stumbled, he reached for the first guy to keep from falling but pulled him down, too.

Harvey dropped to one knee and put the barrel of his pistol against the first man's head, and quietly said, "Don't move, shithead. Don't even blink or wiggle your fingers. You do exactly as I say when I say, and you may just live through this."

Mendez put a knee in the other man's back while placing his pistol against his face, saying, "That goes for you too, sweet cheeks. Robbins, please relieve these guys of their phones and guns."

"Did you get that, Jim?" Harvey said as Robbins gathered everything up. "Now, what do you want us to do with these two very dangerous men?"

"Take them to their car," Jim answered. "Zip-tie them to something in there so they can't cause any trouble. I'll see what the company wants to do with them."

"Mary, is Gene online? If not, please get him," Jim asked as Harvey and the others were manhandling their prisoners to where the Toyota was parked.

"Hang on, I'll let him know you're asking for him," she said. "And your guy is about five minutes from you."

A couple of minutes later Gene came on asking, "Is everything under control?"

"So far," Jim answered. "Harvey and the others have taken the two from the restaurant and are holding them. My guy should be by me in a few minutes, and I'll follow him to the restaurant. Do you still want the first two removed and if so, is there any place special they need to be taken?"

"I'll be right back," Gene told him. "You concentrate on

Jackson, and I'll work with Harvey regarding the disposition of those two."

"Your guy is taking the exit just north of you," Mary announced. "You should see him in less than a minute."

Seconds later, she added, "He's passing your location right now. Do you have him in sight?"

Seeing a single pickup passing with no other vehicles within a hundred feet, Jim motioned for Randy to follow him and said, "I think so. We'll follow him, and you can let us know if he's our man."

"Harvey, are you on?" Gene asked, coming back online.

"Yes, sir," he answered. "What do you want me to do?"

"I just got off the phone with Roadrunner Towing," Gene answered. "They're over on Pecan Drive just off 1518, and they're sending a wrecker to get their car. It's about six miles from you, so if you can keep things under wraps until they arrive, they'll take it from there."

"We can handle it," Harvey told him.

"Your man just passed Schertz Parkway," Mary informed Jim. "You're less than a hundred feet behind him."

"We got him," Jim said, nodding. "General, we may have a slight problem if that wrecker from Roadrunner is there hooking up their car when Jackson arrives. Can you possibly have them wait until I get control of my man?"

"I'll give them another call," he answered. "They'll wait. You get this finished and he may have two cars to tow out of there."

Chapter Fifty-seven

"What do you want us to do while we're waiting?" Harvey asked.

"Do you feel like being a rabbit again?" Jim asked as they tailed Jackson on the service road.

"What this time?" he answered, shaking his head.

"I want you to pretend you're being held by the two you've got in the car," Jim explained. "Make sure their weapons are safe and give them back. But make damn sure they know if they fail to cooperate, they'll be shot immediately."

"Mendez and Robbins, I want you guys to be out of sight on opposite sides of their car," he continued. "Harvey, when we arrive, you'll be standing in front of their car with your hands behind your back as the two guys flank you. You'll be slightly in front of them, so keep your weapon in both hands in case one of them goes stupid and tries to take it. I'm hoping that Jackson won't do anything there in the parking lot but be ready to take care of him if he pulls a weapon," Jim told them. "Mendez, you and Robbins keep your guns trained on the two guys but watch Jackson as he gets out of his pickup. As the General said, let's try to keep this as low profile as possible. We damn sure don't need to have the senior citizens and families spilling out of the restaurant to see an old west shootout."

"Jackson should be taking Universal City Blvd in about two miles," Mary informed them. "That's about three miles from the restaurant. I'd guess that you'll be there in five minutes or so."

"What do you want us to do with Jackson until you get here?" Harvey asked.

"Depends on him," Jim answered as they passed Evans Road and closed the distance between them and Jackson. "If he's a threat, shoot him. If he comes to you with no weapon displayed, put your gun in his face when he gets close and keep him until I arrive. I shouldn't be more than a couple of seconds behind him."

"What's he driving?" he asked as Mendez and Robbins were getting their prisoners out of their car.

"A rust brown pickup," Jim answered as Jackson slowed.

"You're coming up to the exit," Mary broke in. "It's going to be designated Olympia Parkway. It'll make a quick right loop back across I-35 to become Universal City Blvd. You're about four minutes out from the restaurant."

"What do you plan to do when you get here?" Harvey asked as the two men were led up beside him.

"Honestly, I'm not sure," Jim confessed as they made a right turn on Olympia Parkway. "I guess it depends on how many people are around when I get there. How far from the restaurant entrance is their car?"

"It's pretty close to the far end of the parking lot," Harvey answered. "When you pull in, it's down at the south end. I'll guess maybe a hundred feet. Maybe a little more."

"Two minutes," Mary advised them.

"Are you guys ready?" Jim asked. "Are you where Jackson will see you when he pulls in?"

"We're ready," Harvey answered, looking at Mendez and Robbins as they crouched between the sides of the Toyota and the cars beside it.

Turning slightly to look at each of the men by his sides, Harvey told them, "This is it, kids. Don't do anything that'll give those two a reason to blow your meager brains across the parking lot. And if you dare touch me, I'll shove my pistol under your chin and remove the top of your skull."

Staring at them, he continued, "And if you plan on doing anything when your buddy gets here, I'll shoot him in the face while my guys take care of your sorry asses. If you've ever been absolutely sure of anything in your worthless lives, be sure of this. All of you will be left in a pool of blood while we go back into the restaurant and finish our meals."

"One minute," Mary called as they turned right on Pat Booker.

"Get right on his ass when he turns into the parking lot," Jim told Randy. "I'm going to get out as soon as you stop behind him. I'll go to the right side of his pickup. You follow me as soon as you can on the driver's side and concentrate on Jackson. He'll be the only one with a gun, and he may spin around when you slide up to where he just parked. If possible, maybe we can get him before he has a chance to get out. But he may exit with a gun in his hand. If he does and you have a clear shot, take it. Just try not to hit me."

"I've got you in sight," Harvey announced as he saw Jackson's pickup pulling into the lot. "Mendez, you and Robbins be ready to step out from behind the cars and shoot all of these guys if this goes to shit. And please, as Jim just said, try not to hit me."

228

Chapter Fifty-eight

As Randy accelerated to close the gap with Jackson as they entered the parking lot, he was a split second too slow to hit the brakes as the pickup came to a stop just feet from where Harvey was standing.

As their car hit the pickup, knocking it forward, Jim jumped from the still-moving car and ran to the passenger window, pointing his pistol at the shocked Jackson.

"Keep your hands on the wheel," he said as Mendez and Robbins stepped out from between the cars. "Don't try to get out. Don't go for any weapon. Don't reach anywhere. Don't move. Nod if you understand."

Watching him slowly nod, Jim looked toward the restaurant exit and saw a couple of people step out. "Harvey, please go assure those folks it was a minor fender bender, and we're working it out with the driver," he told him. "And have Mendez secure those two and put them back in their car."

"Mary, is Gene still on?" Jim asked as Harvey went toward the people who were staring at the cars.

"I'll get him," she answered.

"I'm on," Gene said seconds later. "What's the status?"

"We still have the first two," Jim answered as Harvey returned. "And I have one very important addition."

"Do you want me to send the tow truck now?" Gene guessed. "Or do you need two trucks?"

Jim looked at Randy and asked, "Is your car drivable?"

"No problem," Randy answered, taking a quick look at the front of the Suburban. "A little dent in the grill, but no real damage. I'll drive it out."

"Just one," Jim told Gene. "I'll take care of the other car.

Harvey, please secure Jackson's hands. I'd hate to have to disrupt the diners again," Jim said. "And then we'll escort him to join his friends."

"What's your plan now?" Gene asked as soon as he had told the Roadrunner tow truck driver to go to the restaurant.

"I'll have the tow truck take Jackson's pickup to his lot," Jim answered, watching Harvey zip-tying his hands together. "Then I'll take these three to the location of your choice for disposition."

"There's a landfill about four miles east of you on 78 John Peterson Blvd," Gene said. "I'll contact the owner and tell him we have a unique addition to his operation. He'll direct you to where he needs additional material."

"In the meantime, tell Mendez and Robbins they're free to leave," Gene directed. "Randy and Harvey will stay until the tow truck gets there and answer any questions if anyone gets curious. It would look suspicious if there wasn't a driver for both of the vehicles involved."

"How will you get back from where you're taking the Toyota with the passengers?" Randy asked as Robbins double-checked that the three were securely bound.

"I'll take care of that," Gene answered for Jim. "Mendez, you and Robbins get out of there. The fewer people there at the scene of the accident, the fewer questions. I just don't want a crowd to gather and start asking questions. Especially if they happen to notice three gentlemen sitting in a car just feet away.

Jim, you head on over to the landfill. Mary will provide directions," Gene continued. "I'll keep monitoring if we're having any trouble. Randy, once the tow truck takes the pickup away, take the Suburban back to the rental agency, and I'll take care of it. Harvey, then you just take your car and go home. Give me a call later, and we'll get to work on getting your family's life back to normal."

Jim walked over to the Toyota and opened the driver's door. Looking in, he said, "I'm going to get everyone out of here. But the rules remain the same. Don't go stupid on me. Just relax and enjoy the drive. When we get to where I'm taking you, it'll all be over. Until then, don't do anything that would cause me to change my mind."

Getting a nod from each, he got in and started the car. As he pulled out of the parking spot and passed by where Harvey and Randy were waiting for the tow truck, Jackson asked, "Where are you taking us?"

"Just a short drive. A couple of miles," Jim answered as Mary told him to make a right turn out of the parking lot onto Pat Booker. "I'll be leaving you as soon as we get there. Ya'll can work out how to get wherever you're going after that."

Chapter Fifty-nine

Pulling into the landfill just after passing the concrete plant, he stopped beside the 'All Drivers Must Sign In' notice posted at a small one-room building that served as the facility security.

When the guard came out with a clipboard, Jim said, "I'm supposed to drop off this car."

"Lashley?" the guard asked, looking at his clipboard. "Dropping off a car?"

"Yes, sir," Jim told him as he pointed his pistol at Jackson beneath his right arm.

"Just follow the road to the back," the guard told him. "We'll take care of it when you get back." Driving down the dirt track, Jackson asked, "Where the hell are we going?"

"Dropping off the car," Jim said, spotting a fresh depression in the land ahead. "You heard the guard."

As he pulled in, Jackson made a lunge for him trying to get his tied hands on Jim's arm. Backhanding him in the face, Jim said, "Try that again, and I'll kill you right here."

"What the hell are you doing with us?" he screamed at Jim, moving back to the side of the seat. "You said you'd leave us here."

Jim stopped putting the car in park and turned off the engine. Turning to look at Jackson, he said, "I am leaving you here. *You* just won't be leaving."

Transferring the gun to his right hand, he turned and fired two shots, killing the men in the rear seat. Then he aimed the pistol at Jackson and said, "I also said you could work out how to get to wherever you're going. Maybe I lied just a little. I don't think you'll be going anywhere. Maybe hell."

"Why?" Jackson pleaded. "What did we ever do to you?"

"Ever been in Fort Worth?" Jim asked, looking into his eyes. "About a year ago with three others? Does any of this sound familiar? You shot someone just outside of the White Elephant Saloon."

As Jackson's expression changed upon realizing who Jim was, he started to speak when Jim said, "Yeah, that was me. And my wife. You only made one mistake. You killed her instead of me." Then he pulled the trigger.

Leaving the pistol on the seat, he opened the door and started walking back to the guard shack. Pulling out his phone, he punched in the number for Gene.

As he answered, he told him, "It's done. The only one left is the man who started this."

"Will that make everything even?" Gene asked. "Never mind. We'll discuss that later. There's a car parked at the gate waiting for you. Drive it back to Denny's and get your car. I'll take care of everything. Just go home. I'll call you tomorrow."

An hour later, Jim was headed north on I-35 when the adrenaline finally subsided. Feeling more tired than he'd ever felt, he saw a sign for the Best Value Motel just past the upcoming exit. Making the decision that he couldn't make it through the traffic in Austin, let alone take three more hours to get home, he took the exit and pulled into the motel's parking lot.

At the front desk, a twenty-something-year-old skinny kid asked, "Good afternoon, sir. How may I help you?"

"Just a room," Jim answered.

"One bed or two?" he asked.

"One," Jim told him. "In the back if possible."

"How many nights, sir," he asked, typing on his computer.

"One," Jim answered.

"Okay, I have a single for one night," he said, handing Jim a key card. "Last room on the right, second floor. How will you be paying, sir."

Jim pulled out his wallet and started to use his credit card but then thought it would be better not to leave a trace of his presence away from home. Handing the kid a hundred-dollar bill, he waited for him to make a change and print a receipt.

Handing Jim the change, he said, "If there's anything you need, just call down. Have a good evening, sir."

Nodding, Jim went back out to move his car to the room when his phone rang. Seeing the number, he answered, "Yes, sir, General. I'm sort of surprised that you're calling. I thought you were going to call me tomorrow."

"I was," Gene told him. "But when Debbie informed me that you had stopped at Austin, I thought I'd better see if anything was wrong. Is there?"

"No," Jim answered. "Just tired. It's been a long day."

"I understand," Gene replied. "Get a good night's sleep, and we'll talk tomorrow."

"Yes, sir," Jim told him as he pulled into the slot in front of the stairs leading to the second floor. "Tomorrow."

Chapter Sixty

The next morning, Jim rose early and took a quick shower while the room's pot brewed a single cup. Out of the shower with a towel around his waist, he turned the TV on to a local station to check traffic status and weather while sipping the almost palatable coffee.

Halfway through the cup, he decided he couldn't take anymore, poured the remainder in the sink, and tossed the Styrofoam cup in the trash.

Pulling on the same clothes from yesterday, he left the room, deciding to attempt to make it past downtown Austin before the traffic became a snarl.

Starting his car, the growl in his stomach reminded him that he hadn't eaten since noon yesterday. Knowing any delays would only make the traffic situation worse; he decided to wait until he was up by US 290, where the traffic began to abate, before looking for a restaurant.

Merging with the commuters hurrying to their jobs in the city, Jim slid to the left lane and accelerated past the cars that were jostling for position at each on or off-ramp. Shaking his head, he once again thanked his lucky stars that Gene had given him the opportunity to become an airline pilot, thus avoiding the nine-to-five daily routine most people faced.

From the jungles of Vietnam to today, the General had stood beside him, guiding his career through counseling and behind-the-scenes manipulation. Even now with his quest for revenge, Gene was steadfast in his support. With one man left, Jim could see the end and knew that Gene would do everything possible to give him the opportunity he desired.

Finally, through the worst of the traffic, he began looking at the towering signs along the highway with the names of various restaurants and motels. Spotting one ahead on the opposite side of I-35 that advertised The Omelettry, he slid to the right and took the exit for Airport Blvd.

After stopping at the intersection and waiting for the light to turn green, he made a left turn, passing beneath I-35, and spotted the restaurant on the right-hand side about a mile up the road.

Parking two slots from the restaurant door, he looked through the glass front and saw a few open tables and several open seats at the counter. Wanting to avoid any social contact, he headed to the left, where he had seen an open table against the wall. Taking a seat, he grabbed the menu and looked at the omelet options.

Settling for the Spanish omelet, he returned the menu to the table and waited for someone to come take his order. Glancing around, he noticed that most of the patrons appeared to be middle-aged working class. No suits or ties. No children. The type of restaurant he found usually has good meals at a reasonable price. And right now, he craved simple. The way he had grown up.

"What'll you have, Hon," the waitress said as she arrived with a glass of water.

"Spanish omelet, home fries, sourdough toast, and black coffee," he answered, smiling at her.

"I'll be right back with the coffee," she said, scribbling on her order pad.

As she was walking away, his phone rang. "Good morning, General," he answered. "I'd ask how you knew I'd be up, but I'd be denying what I know about you and the company."

"Acceptance of reality is the first step to attaining a blissful life, Grasshopper," Gene told him.

"Philosophy before breakfast," Jim responded. "I reckon I should be happy to have such wisdom injected into my otherwise mundane existence."

"So glad I can be of service," Gene replied. "However, that's not the real reason I'm calling."

"First, I want to tell you that I appreciate the way you handled the situation in San Antonio," he continued. "The *accident* was a perfect cover and as low profile as we could ever hope for."

"Before you congratulate me or any of us," Jim interrupted, "The *accident* was truly an accident. It wasn't planned. But it worked out."

"I know it wasn't planned," Gene told him. "I was listening. I'm just saying that you guys took a possibly explosive situation and adapted to a fortunate turn of events. Now, if you'll allow me to continue, I'll tell you why I'm calling."

"Of course, sir," Jim said as the waitress brought his coffee.

"It appears that Lamance has ceased all of his operations here in the States," Gene told him. "We've been monitoring all of the contracts we were aware of and his bids on future contracts. There've been no further bids, and the contracts he's been performing have been reopened for bids."

"I guess that means that our guys can relax with the threat to them removed," Jim surmised. "That's definitely good news."

"Yes, it is," Gene agreed. "We're still closely monitoring all of his operatives here, but the communications have dropped to almost nonexistent. The only thing we've picked up since last night has been attributed to personal use of the phones they were supposed to have destroyed."

"So where does that leave Henry?" Jim asked. "If he's no longer operating here, I'm going to hazard a guess that he's still overseas."

"That's part of what we need to talk about," Gene told him as the waitress returned with his omelet. "But we need to meet here to decide a course of action if you continue to want to fulfill your original desire about everyone involved with Jennifer's death."

Pausing, he continued, "I don't want you to make the decision immediately. But give it some thought when you get home. You've got several days until your next trip, and I'll send the plane down when you're ready. This one will require a lot more than a quick trip to San Antonio or Chicago. Just think about it and give me a call in a couple of days."

"I'll do that," Jim told him as he squeezed some ketchup onto his fries. "Right now, I just want to go home and try to get my normal life back on track. An afternoon of *Little House on the Prairie* sounds about as exciting as I want right now. I'll be in touch."

Chapter Sixty-one

Two days later, Jim called Quantico and waited for Gene to answer. "Good morning, sir," he said as he was transferred to his office. "What's new in the world of international intrigue and clandestine operations?"

"Same as yesterday. Same as last week. Same as forty years ago when the British cracked the Enigma Machine," Gene answered. "Don't know if you remember the Spy Vs Spy cartoons from Mad Magazine, but I've come to believe that our business is a constant battle between equal opponents who both believe they're correct, and we just swap victories when one of us gains some slight advantage for a short period of time."

"Isn't that called job security?" Jim asked, chuckling.

"I suppose," Gene agreed. "Might even be humorous if it wasn't deadly. So, ready to discuss *your* international intrigue situation?"

"Might as well," Jim answered. "If I didn't, I'd feel as if I'd failed my promise to Jennifer. When do you want me to come up?"

"I can have the plane there by noon if you're ready," Gene told him. "We can have dinner this evening and take care of business tomorrow morning. Put you back home tomorrow in time for the latest episode of *Law and Order* while you indulge in a Jack and Coke.”

“Sounds like a plan,” Jim told him. “I’ll pack a quick bag and be at Love Field at twelve o’clock.”

“Good,” Gene responded. “I’ll set the wheels in motion and have a team ready to review our options tomorrow morning. If you don’t mind, I’ll secure you a room here instead of a hotel.”

“That’s good enough for me,” Jim answered remembering how much Jennifer had enjoyed the fine hotels and restaurants when she accompanied him. “I’ll see you this evening.”

Eight hours later, Gene was waiting when Jim came down the steps from the Gulf Stream at Quantico. “Good trip?” he asked, shaking Jim’s hand.

“As good as spending four hours in an airplane could be, I guess,” Jim answered, carrying his single bag to the Suburban. “Certainly a hell of a lot better than the four-hour drive to San Antonio a couple of days ago.”

“You know the average citizen would be impressed with a private jet to whisk them to a secret location to enjoy a fine meal in the company of people whose fingers are on the pulse of exotic matters of state,” Gene said as he got in the car. “And yet you seem immune to the experience.”

“Secret location?” Jim asked as they sped to the gates leading into Black Water Headquarters. “Last time I looked, Quantico, Virginia, was on just about any map you looked at. And a fine meal at the company cafeteria? Debatable. And even I don’t want to get into discussions concerning fingers on the pulse of exotic matters of state. I think it’s more along the lines of a proctologist examination.”

Stopping inside the first set of gates to gain entry, Gene showed his ID and waited until the guard opened the second set.

Once parked, he escorted them into the interior of the headquarters building. "Let's get you settled in your room," Gene said, leading the way down the hall. "Do you need any time other than to toss your bag down and wash your hands?"

"That's all I need," Jim answered as they passed rooms where he had spent numerous nights over the past ten years.

"Who's meeting us for dinner?" he asked moments later as he dried his hands.

"Debbie, Thomas Williams from the Black Water operations division, and William Thomas from Dark Water," Gene answered as they headed back down the hall.

"Thomas Williams and William Thomas?" Jim asked with a quizzical look. "Pseudonyms?"

"Actually… no," Gene answered as they entered the cafeteria. "That's their real names. I wondered the same thing, so I checked."

Spotting Debbie with two men, Gene headed over and introduced them to Jim when they got there, saying, "Tom, Bill, this is Jim Lashley. Jim, meet Tom and Bill."

After shaking hands, Gene said, "You guys sit down, and we'll be right back with a tray. Can I get any of you anything?"

Seeing them shake their heads, he and Jim headed for the buffet line. Once they had filled their trays and returned to the table to join everybody, Bill said, "Jim, I heard that you started out with Dark Water. How'd you enjoy that?"

Pausing before answering, Jim finally said, "I thought the smell of dirty goats, the stench of the scratchy nasty ass dirty robe I'd worn for a week, a pair of sandals made from prickly pear or some other variety of cactus, and the unbelievably foul taste of some ungodly mush made of who knows what part of the dirty goat I'd shared the tent with only two nights ago to be some of the most exotic experiences of my life."

Bill and Tom sat looking at him when they both suddenly burst out laughing, saying, "That was the Five Star tent. You should thank your lucky star that you didn't have to stay in their version of the Best Value Tent accommodations."

Chapter Sixty-two

The next morning, Jim spotted Debbie sitting alone at one of the long tables near the rear of the cafeteria. After getting a breakfast tray with scrambled eggs covered in sausage gravy, four strips of crispy bacon, and a black coffee, he walked to where she was, looking at a stack of papers as she ate.

"Mind if I join you?" he asked before setting his tray down across the table from her.

"Please," she answered, putting the papers back into a file. "How'd you sleep?"

"Like a newborn baby," Jim said, smiling. "Up half the night with dirty diapers crying for Mama."

"That bad, huh?" she asked laughing. "Sounds like you'd rather be back in the tent with a goat." "Okay, it wasn't that bad," he told her, taking a seat. "But I've spent half of my life in a twelve-by-twelve room sleeping on a bed with questionable sheets, and lord knows what gooey substance embedded in the carpet. I'm not comfortable anywhere except my own bed."

"I'm starting to feel that way myself," she said as she pulled a box from her briefcase and slid it across the table.

"What's this?" Jim asked, looking at the box.

"Your old phone," she answered. "It was definitely bugged. More accurately, tapped. But it was so rudimentary, more like some small-town Barney Fife attempt, that all it could do was listen in on a conversation. No tracking. And definitely no capability to monitor off-call communications." Taking it out of the box, he asked, "So, it's clean?"

"As a newborn baby's bottom," she replied. "Without the dirty diapers. And I did a little modification to ensure it can never be tapped or anything else."

"Except by you and the NSA," Jim said, turning it on.

"Oh, the NSA can't touch this one," she exclaimed, taking a drink of her orange juice. "This is what I call Debbie's retirement package. I'd patent it, but then they'd access the patent and appropriate the technology for 'National Security' reasons."

"I thought you worked for the NSA," Jim replied, splashing some Tabasco on the gravy-covered eggs.

"I work with, not for them," Debbie clarified. "I work for Black Water and part of my contract with them is that I retain proprietary control of technology I develop regardless of whether or not they funded my research."

"Smart," Jim agreed, nodding.

"Hey, I've been to three county fairs and two goat ropings," she told him. "Nobody shucks my corn except me."

"I haven't heard that expression since I was knee-high to a stunted cat," Jim said, laughing.

"What's so funny?" Bill said as he and Tom came to the table with trays.

"Just a long-ago country saying," Jim said. "Care to join us?"

"Thanks," Tom said, sitting down beside Jim.

"What have you two been up to since we last saw you?" Debbie asked as Bill sat beside her.

"I'm not sure we should discuss this with you around," Tom answered, looking at her.

"I doubt if either of you can surprise me," she replied. "Give."

Bill looked at Tom and said, "Go ahead. You opened the door."

Tom looked at Debbie and Jim, saying, "Have either of you read or even heard of a book titled 'The Predatory Female' written some years ago by Reverend Lawrence Shannon?"

Seeing both of them shaking their heads, he continued, "Well, my friend Bill has just gone through his third divorce and is contemplating diving back into the proverbial dating pool. I told him to get a copy and read it at least twice before entering into any long-term, or even short-term, commitment.

I, fortunately, was given a copy by my divorce lawyer after my first and only splitting of the assets," he continued. "I argue that any divorce lawyer for the male half of the proceedings should be required by law to include a copy of it along with his final bill."

As Debbie shook her head, Gene walked up, asking, "You aren't giving dating advice again, are you, Tom? I just happened to hear you mention Reverend Shannon, so I know the gist of the conversation from previous ones regarding your opinion of the holy state of matrimony. And statistically speaking, that opinion holds up only fifty percent of the time."

"Which means I'm correct on the other half," Tom added, smiling. "Fifty-fifty is just a flip of the coin. And in my humble opinion, it's always heads you win and tails I lose. Or, in Bill's case, it's lose, lose, lose. And the third time certainly wasn't a charm. I just offer sage advice. Whether or not he heeds it is up to him."

"I'll leave that issue to you two," Gene said, looking at them. "But I believe we have other issues to discuss this morning. So, when you're finished with your breakfast and 'sage' advice, I'll be in the briefing room."

Chapter Sixty-three

Gene was on the phone when they walked into the small briefing room. As the guys took seats, Debbie walked to a podium beside a large wall-mounted screen. Using the computer on the podium, she put a map of Bulgaria on the screen when Gene said, "Debbie, give us an update on Lamance and exactly where he is this morning."

Zooming in, she said, "Henry is still in Bulgaria trying to keep his operations in Europe going. Currently, he's in a small town called Vitanovo near the border with Turkey."

Zooming further in to show the area around the town, she continued, "He contracted with the Bulgarian government to help interdict drugs coming up from Turkey. Currently, he's got roughly a hundred people in the area monitoring roads or other routes where the drugs are being smuggled."

Zooming in again, showing Henry walking down a cobblestone street with a lady by his side, she told them, "We've got a satellite that's synchronized to his phone, and we can visually follow him wherever he goes."

"How much delay is there from the satellite video to us seeing it?" Jim asked.

"Watch this," she said, making several keystrokes. "I've just called his phone."

Seconds later, they watched him stop and take his phone from the robe he was wearing. After looking at the phone's screen, he handed it to the lady with him, and she exchanged it for another one.

"Pretty fast," Jim said, nodding. "What did he just do with the phone?"

"He's paranoid, and for good reason," Debbie explained. "If any unknown call comes in, he tosses the phone and gets a new one. The lady carries several, and she's also the voice on the phone when we monitor his calls."

"Okay," Jim said, looking at Gene. "What does this have to do with me?"

"I want to present you with a couple of options," Gene answered. "That's why Tom and Bill are here, and I'll let Bill brief you on what Dark Water is planning regarding Henry."

Bill rose and walked to the front of the room, saying, "You've just seen how we can track him twenty-four hours a day. I've got a team in Vitanovo ready to remove him within minutes of being given the order. I could make a call, and we could watch the assassination five minutes later, sitting right here. That's the simplest and least costly way to remove him and shut down his entire operation. It's also my choice of action."

Tom rose and walked up to stand beside Bill and said, "This is also my recommendation. I understand your reason for wanting to be involved, but I'm looking at it purely as an assassination using the fewest assets with the greatest chance of success for the company. I'm not considering any personal reasons for deciding what action to take."

As they stood there and Jim continued to watch Henry walking along the street, Gene said, "I've looked at every option. Letting the Dark Water team eliminate him over there. Sending you to join the team in Bulgaria, which Tom says he can do by a temporary reassignment to Dark Water and Bill has said is fine with him. Or bringing Henry back and letting you take care of him here.

Personally, I agree with Tom and Bill from the company's standpoint," Gene said, looking at Jim. "But I gave you my word that I'd support you whatever you wanted to do. As far as I'm concerned, the company will back whatever decision you make."

Jim looked at the screen again, watching the man walking carefree down the street. The very man who had given the order to assassinate him and had been ultimately responsible for his wife's death. After several seconds, he looked up at the four people standing in front of him and simply said, "Bring the son-of-a-bitch here. He dies by my hand."

Chapter Sixty-four

Gene pulled Tom to the side as they were leaving the room and asked, "How long will it take you to get Lamance back here?"

"I can have him here by noon tomorrow," Tom answered. "If that's what you want, I'll get with Bill, and we'll have his team take him within the next ten minutes. I've got a helicopter in Malko Tarnovo that's only about six or seven miles away. I'll get him on his way, and he'll take Lamance and Bill's team to Primorsko.

I've got a Gulf Stream Five in Istanbul that can be there within thirty minutes," he continued. "Given the time difference, noon is definitely doable."

"Start the ball rolling," Gene directed. "Let me know if you run into any snags.'

Returning to where Jim was still sitting watching the screen, Gene said, "Lamance should be here by noon tomorrow. What are your plans then?"

"I need to take him out to a friend's place," Jim answered. "I'll take care of him there."

"If you're talking about Bitterroot's place, I'd like to know exactly what you plan to do with Lamance out there,"

Gene said. "I've had a couple of people do a little digging out there in conjunction with our previous discussions about him and North.

To say the man tends to go for overkill is putting it mildly," he continued. "I'm not going to interfere with whatever you have planned, but getting Bitterroot involved is risky for the company. I'm just asking you to bear that in mind."

Jim sat staring into space for a couple of minutes and finally said, "I started this with a desire to kill everyone involved. I tried to follow the old biblical eye for an eye law. I vowed to shoot each of the shooters in the head as they did Jennifer.

I realize I also killed others in my attempt to follow that principle," Jim admitted. "But they were trying to kill me."

Jim looked up at Gene and explained, "The shooters were merely following orders. They didn't target either me or Jennifer. I was just an assignment; much as I view those people, the company sends me to eliminate.

The only difference between them and me is that I try to avoid collateral damage, especially innocent bystanders," he continued. "Henry is a different matter. He's the reason why Jennifer is dead. He's the reason I lost a year of my life. He deserves what I've planned for him."

"So, you're setting aside the eye for an eye rational?" Gene asked. "Doesn't Mosaic law tell you that the injury an offender inflicts on you should be inflicted on him? That's where the eye for an eye comes from. If you're going to quote it for the shooters, shouldn't that be your guiding principle for everyone involved?

Shouldn't you do the same to him as you did the others?" Gene asked. "I agree that he didn't pull the trigger, but the trigger wouldn't have been pulled except for him. Therefore, he deserves to have the trigger pulled against him.

I believe you have more than a mere trigger pull planned for him," Gene continued. "I know about the Russian boar discussion you and Butch had with Bitterroot. Bitterroot happened to mention something about building a trap to watch some hogs he was trapping demonstrate their viciousness. Particularly involving their carnivorous appetites. He was especially anxious to watch a pair of 400-pound boars with eight-inch snouts, three-inch tusks, and an insatiable taste for blood.

I'm not here to judge your morality, but I've known you for most of your life," Gene said, putting his hand on Jim's shoulder. "I just want you to ask yourself, if you're doing this for Jennifer, what would she think about what you've got planned for Lamance? I'll let you decide that. But I've never seen you harbor such animosity. Ever.

The last thing I'll say is that if that's what you truly want to do, I'll stand behind you," Gene told him. "But you need to remember that some of the things we do never leave us. Both of us have seen things that come back to haunt us. That wakes us up in the middle of the night in a cold sweat. Don't let this be another one."

Just as he was waiting for Jim's answer, Debbie came running back into the room and said, "You've got to see this."

Turning to the screen, they watched as Henry was firing an Uzi Pro pistol at two men standing over a man lying on the ground. Lying beside Lamance was what appeared to be the body of the lady whom they had seen in previous scenes.

"What the hell is going on?" Tom asked, rushing into the room. "Bill just told me his team was involved in a firefight with their target."

As he joined them, watching it play out on the screen, Bill came in with the phone to his ear, shouting, "Then kill the bastard! I don't give a shit about what the previous orders were. I don't want another one of my men dying for this operation. Kill the son-of-a-bitch before he kills another one of you."

Within seconds, they saw Henry's body jerking backward as the rounds struck him in the chest and face. As the two men who had been standing over their fallen comrade approached Lamance's fallen body, one of them pointed his pistol at Henry's head and fired three shots.

As they continued to watch the drama unfold, Bill hung up his phone, turned to Gene, and said, "I'm sorry, sir. But I couldn't let my men risk any more lives. I'll take full responsibility for the failure of the operation."

"I want a full report in the morning," Gene told him, shaking his head. "But, as far as I'm concerned, you and your men made the right decision."

Turning to Tom, he said, "Get the helicopter in there to take care of our man. I want him on the flight back here ASAP."

"What about Lamance?" Tom asked. "Do you want us to bring his body back also?"

Gene looked at Jim and asked, "That's your call. What do you want?"

Jim continued to look at Henry's body as a puddle of blood formed beneath his head for a couple of seconds and finally answered, "No, leave him there. It ends now."

Chapter Sixty-five

The next morning, Jim woke in his own bed. After laying there for a couple of minutes, he rose and padded into the kitchen to start a pot of coffee.

Returning to the bedroom to make the bed and then brush his teeth, he walked back into the kitchen just as the coffeemaker sputtered, sending the last of the boiling water into the basket of Folgers Classic Roast.

Filling his cup, he walked out onto the back porch and sat where he had spent much of the previous night wrestling with the demons that had occupied the deepest corners of his mind before finally heading to bed.

Looking at the empty glass beside the half-empty bottle of Jack Daniel's sitting beside the picture of him and Jennifer that he had carried out there last night, a picture that had been taken at his parent's house so long ago, he sat his cup down and picked up the picture.

Holding it gently in his hands, he softly said, "I loved you when I found you. I loved you when I lost you. And all the days in between.

Now it's finally over. I only hope you'll forgive me for having done what I needed to do. I thought I was doing it for you, but I was actually doing it for me. For that act of selfishness, I ask your forgiveness.

Now, I'll hold you in my heart for all the days to come. Goodbye, my sweet lady. Until I can be with you again."

Setting the picture back on the table, he closed his eyes and leaned back in his chair, knowing that he had done his best and the past had finally been put to rest.